THE B
OF TH
ADIRONDACK
TALES

THE BEST
OF THE
ADIRONDACK
TALES

W. H. H. Murray

Edited and with an Introduction by Randall S. Beach

**EXCELSIOR
EDITIONS**

Published by State University of New York Press
© 2022 State University of New York Press
All rights reserved
Printed in the United States of America

Excelsior Editions is an imprint of State University of New York Press
For information, contact State University of New York Press, Albany, NY
www.sunypress.edu

Library of Congress Cataloging-in-Publication Data

Names: Murray, W. H. H., author
  Edited and with an introduction by Randall S. Beach
Title: The best of the Adirondack tales
Description: Albany : State University of New York Press [2022] |
  Series: New York Classics; Excelsior Editions
Identifiers: ISBN 9781438490557 (hardcover : alk. paper) |
  ISBN 9781438490564 (e-book) | ISBN 9781438490540
  (paperback : alk. paper)
Further information is available at the Library of Congress.

10 9 8 7 6 5 4 3 2 1

Contents

Introduction

Randall Beach

William Henry Harrison Murray is best known for his 1869 work *Adventures in the Wilderness or Camplife in the Adirondacks*. That book and the lecture series that followed introduced the urban public of the nineteenth century to the wonders of spending time in the wilderness and led to a tourism rush into the Adirondacks that lasted several years. The "Murray Rush" and the basic philosophy of nature that Murray espoused had a profound impact on outdoor life and has led some to regard Murray as the father of the outdoor movement and the vacation in America.

Murray was born in Guilford, Connecticut, on April 26, 1840. His childhood was spent reading, working, and, perhaps most tellingly, exploring the countryside surrounding the family homestead. Murray attended Yale University, graduating in 1862, and later the East Windsor Hill Seminary. As a Congregationalist minister in Connecticut, his oratorical abilities were honed, and in 1869, the twenty-nine-year-old was asked to become the minister of the famed Park Street Church in Boston, Massachusetts. Murray's larger-than-life personality shone in Boston, often against the wishes of his more conservative congregation. His passions included camping in the Adirondacks, hunting and fishing, and, perhaps worst of all in the eyes of his church, horses.

After leaving Park Street Church in 1874, W. H. H. Murray started his own church in Boston, invested in a wagon company, went bankrupt, traveled, lectured, and lived for various periods of time in San Antonio, Texas; Montreal, Quebec; and Burlington, Vermont. Eventually, Murray returned to his childhood home in Guilford, Connecticut, and there, with his second wife, devoted his remaining years to raising his four beloved daughters.

His circle became complete in 1904 when Murray died in the same room that he had been born in some sixty-four years before.

While *Adventures* was Murray's first book, it was far from his last. From 1869 to his death in 1904, Murray wrote and published many works. His subsequent books included tomes on breeding horses, the deficiencies of deacons, Lake Champlain and yachting, traveling across Canada, and education. His written work reflects his many passions, which he ever sought to share with the public, and his evolution as a preacher, thinker, and man in late nineteenth-century America.

Murray's passions were many, but the Adirondack Mountains always remained foremost. For years he camped in the Raquette Lake area and traveled, usually by boat, throughout the New York wilderness. His lecture on the Adirondacks was presented more than five hundred times, and *Adventures* appeared in numerous printings and editions. Beginning in 1870, Murray began to compile and publish a collection of his short stories regarding the Adirondacks, as his *Adirondack Tales*. *Adirondack Tales* was published and sold, eventually by subscription only, throughout the later years of the nineteenth century. Comprising five volumes in all, the collection includes short stories, two longer novellas entitled *The Doom of Mamelons* and *Ungava*, and several of the lectures Murray had presented along the way.

It was within the stories presented in *Adirondack Tales* that Murray introduced his readers to three characters who took center stage in most of his wilderness stories: John Norton the Trapper, Henry Herbert, and the Lad (aka the Man Who Didn't Know Much). John Norton the Trapper was, for Murray, the prototypical "old-school, New England man." He was a man completely at one with nature and the wilderness. According to Murray, the character came about after a dinner with his publisher and other authors at which Ralph Waldo Emerson asserted that a good story required the inclusion of a female character, as sentimentality was impossible without one. Of that encounter, Murray tells us, "I was compelled to say that I did not see the need of introducing a woman into every story . . . and that in some masculine natures was a tenderness as deep, a sympathy as sweet, and a love as strong as existing in woman." At the urging of his publisher, Murray took up this challenge and the result was John Norton.

Henry Herbert, an urban sportsman who befriends John Norton, is an avatar of Murray. Herbert is everything one would expect from a nineteenth-century city gentleman. He is well-educated and well-mannered. Herbert is also a lover of the wilderness and has gained a reputation as such. He is as at home in a canoe or on shore with a long rifle as he is back home in his genteel dining room. Herbert is the well-rounded, complete individual that Murray thought all should strive to be.

Finally, the man known only as the Lad, or the Man Who Didn't Know Much, is a character that exudes innocence and simplicity. He becomes friend and companion to both Norton and Herbert. The Lad joins the pair in many adventures and brings the wisdom of innocence with him, offering both characters and the reader lessons in the virtue of humility and kindheartedness.

At the heart of this compilation, four stories feature John Norton, Henry Herbert, and the Lad. In "The Story That the Keg Told Me," Norton and Herbert have their first meeting on the shores of a desolate Adirondack lake. There Murray spins a tale around the two men that focuses on the theme of redemption through time in the wilderness. The redemptive nature of the woods is a theme touched on again and again in Murray's writings and is made in reference to spiritual, mental, and physical health.

"Henry Herbert's Thanksgiving" takes the Trapper and the Lad out of the wilderness and into the genteel Boston home of Henry Herbert. In this holiday story, Murray stresses the joy and importance of brotherly love and the honor of service to others. It is also in this tale that Murray subtly explores Henry Herbert as the ideal, well-rounded man. Herbert's home, filled with both nineteenth-century Victorian luxuries and the trophies of a man well-familiar with wilderness adventure, is described as a strange conjunction of the semibarbaric and effeminate. Throughout the *Adirondack Tales*, we find that Henry Herbert represents a similar conjunction. The out-of-place Trapper is also used by Murray to again draw the reader's attention to the power of the natural world versus the very unnatural urban environment. Norton, when speaking to Henry about the inhumane poverty the Trapper has witnessed in the city, reminds his friend that "yer eye gits keen in the woods, but the settlements blind ye."

"The Ball" is actually a chapter excerpted from the longer story of "The Story of the Man Who Didn't Know Much," in which Murray introduces Norton and Herbert and the reader to the eponymous Lad. The chapter is included here as another good example of Murray's play upon the interaction between the "civilized" world and the "natural world." Here the Lad's fiddle-playing allows Murray to express the transformational qualities of music when it comes from a place of pure innocence and genuine emotion. The story also provides more insight into the character of Murray's prototypical New England man: John Norton. The author tells us that "his nature had within its depths that fine capacity which enabled it to receive the brightness of surrounding happiness and reflect it again," and "the man of the woods, of the lonely shore, and of silence, seemed perfectly at home amid the noise and commotion of human merry-making."

The last of the Norton/Herbert/Lad stories included in this volume is the story entitled "How John Norton the Trapper Kept His Christmas." This story was included in the book *Holiday Tales*, published by Murray, and focuses on the events of John Norton's Adirondack Christmas. While Henry Herbert and the Lad appear only in abstention, Murray uses Norton's adventure to drive home the true meanings of Christmas, that of charity and love.

"Freemasonry of Outdoor Life" was originally published as part of Murray's supplemental notes to his *Mamelons* and *Ungava* stories that comprised the fourth volume of *Adirondack Tales*. It is included here as a succinct expression of the esteem Murray placed on both the natural world and its abilities to aide humankind.

Finally, "Jack Shooting in a Foggy Night" is included as an example of the humorous stories that Murray peppered both *Adventures in the Wilderness* and *Adirondack Tales* with. While the story originally appeared in *Adventures*, Murray apparently liked it enough to publish it again as part of volume 4 of *Adirondack Tales*. It is a silly story in which Murray is the narrator. Like all of the stories that were originally included in *Adventures*, Murray has left it to his readers to decide whether "Jack Shooting" is true account or fable.

The words included in this collection were first written well over one hundred and forty years ago by a man convinced of the importance of interaction between man and nature. Murray believed that the complete and healthy individual combined elements of both the natural and educated world. He recognized the curative powers that time in the wilderness had for nineteenth-century urban dwellers who faced the daily tribulations of rapid industrialization. At their core, these stories remain relevant in today's frantic world filled with distractions that Murray could not begin to imagine. While the negative impacts of the industrial revolution that plagued the cities of Murray's America have been largely abated, today our too-hurried lives face constant bombardment from the distractions of high technology. It is not hard to imagine William Henry Harrison Murray's cure for our modern ills: "Put the screen down, leave the virtual behind, get off the couch and get into the woods."

I leave you reader with the words of my great-great grandfather:

To all that camp on shores of lakes, on breezy points, on banks of rivers, by sandy beaches, on slopes of mountains, and under green trees anywhere, I an old camper, a wood lover, an aboriginal veneered with civilization, send greeting. I thank God for the multitude of you; for the strength and beauty of you; for the healthiness of your tastes and the naturalness of your natures. I eat and drink with you; I hunt and fish with you; I boat and bathe with you; and with you by day and night enjoy the gifts of the good world. Kneeling on the deck of my yacht, stooping far over and reaching low down to fill to the brim the old camping cup that longer than lives of some of you has never failed my lips, and holding it high in the bright sunlight I swing it to the circle of the horizon and standing, bare-headed, with the strong wind in my face, I drink to your health, O campers, whoever and wherever ye be. Here's health to you all and long life on the earth and something very like camping ever after.

—W. H. H. Murray

1

SLEEPING IN THE WOODS

From "Lake Champlain and Its Shores."

Imagine your bed-chamber of odorous bark, and your bed of pungent boughs. Your couch made under murmuring trees and within a few yards of the lazily moving water, whose motions caress rather than chafe the shore. Stretched your full length on such a couch, spread in such a place, the process of falling asleep becomes an experience. You lie and watch yourself to observe the gradual departure of your senses. Little by little you feel yourself passing away. Slowly and easily as an ebbing tide you begin to pass into the dim and insensible realm beyond the line of feeling. At last a moment comes in which you know you are passing over the very verge of consciousness. You are aware that you are about to fall asleep. Your cheek but partially interprets the cool pressure of the night wind; your ears drowsily surrender the lingering murmur of beach and pine; your eyes droop their lids little by little; your nose slightly senses the odor of the piny air, as you mechanically draw it in; the chest falls as it passes as mechanically out, and then—you are asleep.

The hours pass, and still you sleep on. The body, in obedience to some occult law of force within the insensible frame, still keeps up its respirations; but you are somewhere—sleeping. At last the pine above you, in the deep hush which precedes the coming of dawn, stills its monotone, and silence weaves its airy web amid the motionless stems. The water falls asleep. The loon's head is under its spotted wing, and the owl becomes mute. The deer has left the shore, and lies curved in its mossy bed. The rats no longer draw their tiny wake across the creek, and the frogs have ceased their croaking. All is quiet. In the profound quiet, and unconscious of it all, the sleeper sleeps. What sleep such sleeping is! and what a ministry is being ministered unto mind and body through the cool, pure air, pungent with gummy odors, and strong with the smell of the sod and the root-laced mould of the underlying earth!

2

THE FREEMASONRY OF OUTDOOR LIFE

What a splendid Freemasonry this is of the outdoor life! How gentle and generous its rivalries! Which head shall dive deepest in the cool depths or speck the white surf farthest from shore? Which rod shall lift the heaviest trout, or gun show to its credit the fullest bag of game? Whose deck shall shine the cleanest, or whose white sails shall lead the fleet to evening's anchorage? Whose table of bark shall boast of the tenderest venison, or lodge front display for ornament the noblest spread of antlers? Whose rifle is truest to the camp when food is scarce, or is silent longest when game is plenty and the larder over-full? These are the generous and healthy rivalries of the outdoor life which stimulate but never fret, and leave both victor and vanquished healthy and happy still. Compare with these the scramble for wealth; the rivalries for gain; the suicidal despair of some; the vain and boastful bearing of others; the bitterness and ruin of those who lose; the arrogance of those who win; the sneering envyings and rankling jealousies, ripening to hatred as the years go on, which characterize the lives men live in store, office, and street, and note the contrast. Who of us frank-spoken and kind-hearted vagabonds of tide and field, of deck and camp, are envious of any? Each man we meet is comrade, fellow-picnicker, brother-man, partner of ours in the sweet profits of our healthy, happy, natural life. Mild mannered and light-hearted wanderers; boys with smooth or wrinkled faces; gray headed some of us, but boys still, thank God; disciples of the rod and gun; lovers of oar and sail; canoeists, campers, yachtsmen, our fires are lighted on a thousand shores, and our evening song floats over a thousand lakes and island studded rivers. We are a family of nature's saints. Our spirits have been touched and softened by the sweet grace of nature. We have been indoctrinated in the truths that shine out of stars and which the blue heavens declare at noon and night. The leaves of the Catechism we have studied have been the flowery meadows, the voiceful slopes of mountains, the shining beaches, the whispering leaves of trees, the thunder-shaken firmament, or the star-lighted depth of level waters. From these un-Calvinistic text-books we have learned sweet lessons of God, whose gentleness we saw in the very leaves we studied. Our souls have drank the waters of life, fresh from native fountains, and our spirits have bathed their scars in rivers which flow from Him whose voice is as the sound of many waters. All hail! ye healthy bodied, healthy minded, kindly hearted, gentle mannered saints of flood and field, of hill and river, of oar and sail, of deck and camp; your smiling faces rise before me in thousands, and your voices, in happy talk, in joke and song, come from far and stir the silence around me into laughter.

Joke, laugh and rest on, ye thrifty vagabonds and gentle loafers; into each hour you are storing the honey of health, on which in future days of toil and strain your strength shall feed and fill itself with vigor. I hail you, fellow saints in this lower heaven of God's where each happy worshiper is his own priest, each pure mind its own creed, and the gentle wishes of each heart the sum and substance of doctrine.

3

JACK-SHOOTING IN
A FOGGY NIGHT

We were camping on Constable Point, John and I, in the summer of 1868, when the following experience befell me. I tell it because it represents one phase of Adirondack life, and because it will enable me to enjoy over again one of the most ludicrous and laughable adventures which ever assisted digestion.

It was the 8th of July, and a party of Saranac guides, consisting of Jim McClellan, Stephen Martin, and a nephew of his, also a Canadian, name unknown, at least unpronounceable by me, had come up from the Lower Saranac, and were going through to Brown's Tract for a party of German gentlemen (and gentlemen in the best sense of the word we afterward found them to be), who had arranged the year before to camp on the Racquette for a while. The guides were instructed to select and build a camp as they came through, and then, leaving one of their number to keep it, to come after the party, who were to await them at Arnold's. The spot the guides selected was only some twenty rods to the north of us, and there they pitched their tent, close by the little projection of yellow sand which thrusts itself out into the deep blue waters of the lake. The following morning all the guides save the elder Martin started for Arnold's, leaving him to keep camp. Soon after dark Martin, having put everything in order to receive the party, dropped over to our lodge, in the door of which John and I were sitting, smoking our pipes, and chatting of this or that, as men will in the woods.

"Well," said I to Martin, as he came up, "I suppose you have all your arrangements made for the party tomorrow."

"Yes," returned he. "I don't know as I can do much more; only I do wish I could have a big buck hanging by his gambrels when they come pulling in. It would please Mr. Schack mighty well, I tell you. The fact is," he continued, "I came over here to see if you didn't want to go out to-night with your jack. We might take a short stretch up Marion River there, and I think find a venison without much trouble." Of course I was ready to go. Indeed, I was exceedingly glad of the chance. The fact is, one deer a week was all John and I could manage to dispose of; and as I never permit myself to shoot more than the camp can eat or give away, and as no parties had as yet come in, I had very little sport, and eagerly hailed the opportunity which Martin's proposition gave me of "drawing it fine" on a deer's head once more.

So it was settled that we should go jack-shooting up Marion River; and, after a few minutes of further conversation as to our outfit, Martin left to prepare his boat. I proceeded to discharge my rifle, which was loaded with conical balls, in order to recharge with round ones, which are far better for short range and night work.

Perhaps, as a matter of interest to sportsmen, and for the information of the uninitiated reader, I should pause a moment in my narration to describe, not only "jack-shooting," but also "my jack."

Be it known to all, then, that a deer is a very inquisitive as well as a timid animal. His curiosity is generally greater than his timidity, and at the sight of anything new or strange he is impelled by this feeling to inspect it. Hence it is that, instead of flying from a blazing torch or lighted candle at night, he is more apt to stand stock still and gaze at it. Hunters avail themselves of this peculiarity, and hunt them by torchlight in the night-time. Ordinarily speaking, they take a piece of bark some two feet long by ten inches wide, and, bending it into the shape of a half-moon, tack it to a top and bottom board of the same shape. Into this box of bark, shaped like an old-fashioned half-moon lantern, they insert one or more candles, and fasten it to a stick some three feet in length. The stick is then stuck into the bow of the boat, and the "jack" is ready. The hunter, rifle in hand, seats himself close behind and under the jack, and the paddler at the other end of the boat or canoe. Thus equipped they start out. The guide paddles quietly along, until a deer is heard feeding, as is their custom at night, upon the edge of the bank, or walking in the water nipping off the lily-pads, which they love exceedingly. The jack is then lighted and the boat run swiftly down toward the deer. If he is young, or has never seen a jack before, he will let the boat (which he does not see, so intently is he gazing at the light) come very near him, and he is easily shot. If he is old and shy, it is a far more difficult task to get near him. The defects of this jack are evident. It is worthless on any but a perfectly still night, for the least current of air will blow the light out. It necessitates also the scratching of a match previous to "lighting up," and the noise incident to such an operation in the open air at night, when every object about you is damp and wet, and in the presence of game, does not tend to steady the nerves of an amateur. It is also stationary, and if you run past the deer, as you are liable to do, it is difficult to turn the light on him. If, furthermore, the deer is in motion in any but a straight line from you, the jack is of no service at all. Now, when deer are scarce and shy, or the nights windy, such a jack is almost useless, and the sportsman is often driven to change his camp or starve, although deer are all around him. Having in seasons previous experienced the disadvantages of the old jack, I determined to invent and construct one which should absolutely overcome all these imperfections. This is what I hit upon. I took a common fireman's hat, and, having the rim removed, had the crown padded with wadding, and lined with chamois-skin. I caused a half-moon lantern of copper to be made with a concave bottom which fitted closely to the hat, and was fastened thereto with screws. Through the top of the hat a hole was made large enough for the burner to pass; the lamp itself, containing the oil, was fitted and held by brass studs to the crown, between it and the head. In the back side of the lantern was placed a German-silver reflector, heavily plated. The screw which lifts and lowers the wick was connected with a shank that projected through the side of the lantern, so that by a touch of the finger the light might be let on or cut off. A large, softly padded throat-latch buckled the jack firmly to my head. Observe the advantages of this jack over the old style. Being enclosed by an air-tight glass front, it might be used in a tornado. When floating for deer you could turn the wick so low down that no light was visible, and when one was heard you could run down toward him, and, with your finger on the adjusting screw, turn on the light just when you wanted it, and not an instant before, and this too without a moment's pause. If the deer was on the jump, it made no difference. The reflector was so powerful, that, if you turned the wick well up, it made a lane some three rods wide and fifteen rods long as light as day, and the jack being on your head, the blaze was never off the leaping deer, whose motion your eye would *naturally* follow, and as your head turned, so, without thought or effort on your part, turned the jack. Moreover, as all hunters know, one trouble with the old style of jacks is, that as you hold your rifle *under* it, when taking aim, only the *front* sight is lighted up; and the rear sight being in the dark, you cannot "draw it fine," but are ever liable to "shoot over." Shooting with the old style is but little better than *guess* shooting, any way. To be sure, you might discard the rifle, and with an old blunderbuss, charged with slugs or buck-shot, which scatter twenty feet in going forty, get your deer. But this is simply slaughter,—a proceeding too shameful for a sportsman ever to engage in. A man who drops his deer with anything but a single bullet should be hooted out of the woods. Now the jack I am describing, when placed firmly on the head, casts its light from lock to muzzle, and so enables the hunter to draw his bead as "fine" as he may choose. Nothing need be said in favor of this jack,—which is here for the first time described, and thus made common property,—beyond the fact that, during the whole season in which I hunted, mostly nights, I never marked a deer with a bullet back of the ears, unless he was on the jump when I shot. And time and again, as John Plumbley and many friends can testify, on nights good, bad, and indifferent, sitting, kneeling, or standing in the bow of a tottlish boat, I have sunk my bullet as squarely between the eyes as one may place his finger. One word more touching the advantages of this jack. All my readers who have hunted deer at night know that full one half of them started will go out of the river on a jump, and, when ten or twelve rods from the bank, come to a stand-still. Now this distance is too great for an old-style jack to illuminate; and often the hunter must signal his guide to paddle on, when he knows the buck he wants stands not a dozen rods away, looking straight at him. Now, with the aid of a reflector, my jack will throw a lane of light from fifteen to twenty rods; and if the deer stops within that distance, as three out of five will, and you hold steady, he is sure to come into your boat. Never shall I forget an old buck I laid out one night up South Inlet, on the Racquette, as he stood with his nose stuck into the air and blowing away like an animated trumpet. It was just seventeen rods from the bow of the little shell I stood in, and the lead went in at one ear and came out of the other.

So much for jack-shooting and my jack. I have been thus minute in my description, because I thought it might assist my brother sportsmen to enjoy what I regard the most exciting of all sport,— deer-shooting at night. I take this way also of answering the many letters of inquiry concerning my jack recently addressed me by gentlemen who have heard of my invention from the guides, and who would like to avail themselves of it. It is rather expensive, but a *sure* thing, if well made.

Well, to return to my narration. I was driving the ball into the right barrel of my rifle when I heard the soft dip of a paddle abreast of the camp, and in a moment Martin stepped up the bank and entered, paddle in hand, the circle of the firelight. Many who read this may remember Martin, brother to him of the Lower Saranac House; but for the sake of others, who have never seen him, I will give a sketch of him. I recall him perfectly as he stood leaning on his paddle in my camp that night. A tall, sinewy man he was, in height some six feet two, in weight turning perhaps one hundred and seventy pounds,—every ounce of superfluous flesh "sweated" off his body by his constant work at the paddle and oars, which gave him a certain gaunt, bony look, to be seen only in men who live the hunter's life and eat the hunter's fare along our frontiers. Yet there was a certain litheness about the form, a springy elasticity in the moccasined foot, a suppleness of motion, which, if it was not grace, was something next akin to it. His hair was sandy, short, crisp, and curly. His shoulders were brought the least trifle forward, as boatmen's generally are, and especially such as leave their boats to follow, with cat-like tread and crouching posture, the trail. Pants and hunting-shirt of Scotch gray, a soft felt hat of similar color, and the inevitable short, thin knife stuck in a leathern sheath, made up his outfit. A wiry, nervous man, I said to myself, as I looked him over; none the less nervous because a certain backwoodsman's indifference and *nonchalance* veiled the dash and fire within. A good guide I warrant, easy and pleasant of temper when fairly treated, but hot and violent as an overcharged and smutty rifle when abused.

"Martin," said I, as I dragged my jack from under a bag where it had lain concealed (for I did n't wish every one to copy my invention the first season), "what do you think of that?" and, touching a match to the wick, I lifted the jack to my head and buckled the throat-latch.

"Well," said he, after looking at it a moment, "that's a new idea, anyway. Shouldn't wonder if it worked; but I have seen so many new-fangled notions brought into the woods that were not worth a toadstool, that I have about given up ever seeing anything better than a piece of bark, and a tallow dip, mean and tricky as that is."

"Well," said I, moistening my finger and lifting it into the air, "if that current of wind comes out of the north, we shall want something better than a tallow dip to see through the fog with before ten o'clock."

"That's the fact," broke in John; "I saw, an hour ago, by the way that hard maple brand snapped and glowed, that it was getting colder. By the time you reach the river the fog will be thick enough to cut, and the best thing you can do, both of you, is to bunk in here with me, and help me lessen this bag of 'Lone Jack.'"

"No," said I, "fog or no fog, we'll go out. I know how much it would please the party tomorrow to see a good buck hanging in front of the camp as they come down the lake; and, Martin, if you will do your part at the paddle, I'll show you how Never Fail acts when a deer stands looking into the muzzles"; and I patted the stock of my double rifle, of which it is enough to say that it has "N. Lewis, Troy, N. Y.," etched on either barrel.

"Well," replied Martin, as he turned toward the beach, "it's thirty-five years since I raised the first blister on these hands with a paddle-staff, and though it is a mighty silent paddle that is usually back of you, yet we Saranac boys don't admit that any man in this wilderness can beat us in a still hunt."

With this allusion to John's reputation at the paddle, he headed his long, narrow boat out into the lake, and steadied it between his knees until I was seated in the bow; then, with a slight push, sent the light shell from the beach, vaulting at the same instant, with a motion airy as a cat's, into his own seat astern.

Who that has ever visited the Adirondacks does not grow enthusiastic as he recalls the beauty and solemn splendor of the night, as he has beheld it while being paddled across some one of its many hundred lakes? The current of air which I had noted at the camp, cool and refreshing after the hot summer's day, was too steady and slight to stir a ripple on the glassy water. The sky was in its bluest tint, sobered by darkness. In the southern heavens, and even up to the zenith, the stars were mellow and hazy, shorn of half their beams by the moist atmosphere through which they shone. A few, away to the south, over the inlet of that name, lying back of a strata of air saturated almost to the density of vapor, beamed like so many patches of illuminated mist. But far to the north and west, whence at intervals a thin gleam of lightning shone reflected from some far-off nether region, the low growl of thunder was occasionally heard. Above, in the clear, cool blue, the star which never moves, the Dipper, and countless other orbs, differing in glory, revealed in sharp, clear outlines their stellary formations. The waveless water was to these heavens a perfect mirror; and over that seamless surface, over planets and worlds shining beneath us, over systems and constellations the minutest star of which was visible we softly glided. With bowed head I gazed into that illuminated sea. I thought of that other sea which is "of glass like unto crystal" before the throne, and the glory which must forever be reflected up from its depths. "Is this the same world of cities and cursing in which I lived a week ago?" I said to myself, "or have I been translated to some other and happier sphere?" Around me on all sides, as I gazed, Night dusky and dim sat on the mountains, and brooded over the starry sea, and the all-enveloping silence of the wilderness rested solemnly over all. As I sat and mused,—yea, and worshipped,—memory stirred within me; the words of the Psalmist came to my lips, and I murmured, "This is night which showeth wisdom, and the melody of which has gone out through all the world."

My meditations were somewhat rudely interrupted by the grating of lily-pads against the sides of the boat. We had crossed the lake, and were entering the river. My mood changed with the change of locality. The lover of nature was instantly lost in the sportsman, and as we shot into the fog, which, rising above the river, from the lake looked like a great fleecy serpent twined

amid the hills, eye and ear were all alert to detect the presence
of game. But we were doomed to delay. For nearly two miles we
crept through the damp and chilly fog, hearing nothing to inter-
rupt the profound silence save the occasional plunge of a muskrat
or the sputter of a frog skating along the surface of the water. But
all of a sudden, when heart and hope were about to fail, some
distance ahead of us we heard the well-known sounds, k-splash,
k-splash, and knew that a deer, and a large one too, was making
for the shore. Here our adventures began. I signalled Martin, by
a desperate "hitch" on the thwart, to run the boat at full speed
toward the sound. He did. The light shell shot through the fog,
and when in swift career struck the bank, bow on. Martin was tremendous at the paddle, and a little more force would have divided
that marsh from side to side; as it was, the thin, lath-like boat
was buried a third of its length amid the bogs and marsh-grass.
With much struggle, and several suppressed but suggestive exclamations from Martin, we extricated the boat from the meadow
and shoved out into clear water. We had heard nothing from the
deer since he left the river. Thinking that possibly he might have
stopped, after gaining the bank, to look back, as deer often do, I
rose slowly in the boat, turned up the jack, and peered anxiously
into the fog. The strong reflector bored a lane through the fleecy
mass for some fifty feet, perhaps; even at that distance objects
mingled grotesquely with the fog. At the extreme end of the
opening I detected a bright, diamond-like spark. What was it? I
turned the jack up, and I turned it down. I lowered myself until
my eyes looked along the line of the grass. I raised myself on
tiptoe. Nothing more could be seen. "It may be the eye of a deer,
and it may be only a drop of water, or a wet leaf," said I to myself.
Still it looked gamy. I concluded to launch a bullet at it anyway.
Whispering to Martin to steady the boat, I sunk my eye well down
into the sights, and, holding for the gleam amid the marsh-grass,
fired. The smoke, mingling heavily with the fog, made all murky
before me, while the explosion, striking against the mountains
on either side, started a dozen reverberations, so that we could
neither see nor hear what was the result of the shot. After waiting in silence a few moments, hoping to hear the deer "kick,"
without any such happy result, I told Martin I would go ashore
to load, and see what it was I had shot at. He paddled forward,

and, seizing the tall grass, while he forced the boat in against the bank with his paddle, I clambered up. Being curious to ascertain what had deceived me, I strode off into the marsh some forty feet, and, turning up the jack, lo and behold a dead deer lay at my feet! "Martin," shouted I, "here the deer is, dead as a tick!"

"The d—l!" exclaimed the guide from the fog.

"What did you say?" again I shouted.

"I said I did n't believe it," returned Martin, soberly.

"Paddle your canoe up here, then, you old sceptic, and see for yourself," I rejoined, taking the deer by the ear and dragging him to the bank. "Here he is, and a monster too." Martin did as directed. "Well," exclaimed he, as he unbent his gaunt form from the curve into which two hours of paddling had cramped it, and straightened himself to his full height, until his eyes rested upon the buck,—"well, Mr. Murray, you are the first man I ever saw draw a fine bead in a night like this, standing in the bow of a Saranac boat, at the twinkle of a deer's eye, and *kill*. That jack of yours is a big thing, and no mistake." By the time he had finished, the boat had drifted off into the river,—for the current was quite strong at that point,—and I was alone. I was just fitting a cap to the tube of the recharged barrel, when I felt a movement at my feet, and, casting my eyes downward, I saw that the deer was in the act of *getting up!* The ball, as we afterward discovered, had glanced along the front of the skull, barely creasing the skin. It had touched the bone slightly, and stunned him so that he dropped; but beyond this, it had not hurt him in the least. Quick as thought, I put my foot against his shoulder and pushed him over. "Martin," I cried, "this deer isn't dead; he's trying to get up. What shall I do?"

"Not dead!" exclaimed he, shouting from the middle of the river through the dense fog.

"No, he is n't dead; far from it. He is mighty lively, and getting more and more so," I returned, now having my hands full to keep the deer down. "Come out and help me. What shall I do?"

"Get hold of his hind leg; I'll be with you in a minute," was the answer.

I did as directed. I laid hold of his left hind leg, just above the fetlocks, and sprang to my feet.

Reader, did you ever seize a pig by the hind leg? If so, multiply that pig by ten; for every twitch he gives, count six; lash a big lantern to your head; fancy yourself standing alone on a swampy marsh in a dark, foggy night, with a rifle in your left hand, and being twitched about among the bogs and in and out of muskrat-holes, until your whole system seems on the point of a separation which shall send you in a thousand infinitesimal parts in all directions, like fragments of an exploding buzz-wheel, and you have my appearance and feelings as I was jerked about that night amid the mire and marsh-grass, as I clung to the leg of that deer. Now, when I fasten to anything, I always expect to hold on. This was my determination when I put my fingers round that buck's leg. I have a tremendous *grip*. My father had before me. With his hands at a two-inch auger-hole in the head of a barrel, I have seen him clutch, now with his right, now with his left hand, twenty-two house-rats as they came darting out to escape, the stick with which I was stirring them up, and dash them dead upon the floor, without getting a single bite; and everybody knows that a rat, in full bolt, comes out of a barrel like a flash of lightning. I fully expected to maintain the family *prestige* for grip. I did. I stuck to that deer with all my power of arm and will. I felt it to be a sort of personal contest between him and myself. Nevertheless, I was perfectly willing at any time to let go. I had undertaken the job at the request of another, and was ready to surrender it instantly upon demand. I shouted to Martin to get out of that boat mighty quick if he wanted to take his deer home, for I shouldn't hold on to him much longer. It took me about two minutes to deliver that sentence. It was literally jerked out of me, word by word. Never did I labor under greater embarrassment in expressing myself. In the mean while Martin was meeting with difficulty. The bank of the river was steep, and the light cedar shell, with only himself in it, was out of all balance, and hard to manage. It may be that his very strong desire to get on to that meadow where I was holding his deer for him operated to confuse and embarrass his movements! He would propel the boat at full speed toward the bank, then jump for the bow; but his motion forward would release the boat from the mud, and when he reached the bow the boat would be half-way across the river again. Now Martin is a man of great patience. He is not by any means a profane person. He had always shown great respect for the cloth. But everybody will see that his position was a very trying one. Three several times, as he afterward informed me, did he drive that boat into the bank, and three several times, when he got to the bow, that boat was in the middle of the river. At last Martin's patience gave way, and out of the fog came to my ears ejaculations of disgust, and such strong expletives as are found only in choice old English, and howls of rage and disappointment that none but a guide could utter in like circumstances. But human endurance has a limit. I was fast reaching a condition of mind when family pride and transmitted powers of resolution fail. What did I care for my father's exploit with the rats at the two-inch auger-hole? What did the family grip amount to after all? I was fast losing sight of the connection such vanities sustained to me. I was undergoing a rapid change in many respects,—of body as well as mind! When I got hold of that deer's leg, I was mentally full of pluck and hope; my hunting-coat, of Irish corduroy, was whole and tightly buttoned. Now, mentally, I was demoralized; every button was gone from the coat, and the right sleeve hung disconnected with the body of the garment. The jack had been jerked from my head, and lay a rod off in the marsh-grass. I could hold on no longer. I would make one more effort, one more appeal. I did. "Martin," said I, "aren't you EVER going to get out of that boat?"

The heavy thug of the boat against the bank, an explosive and sputtering noise which sounded very much like the word "damn" spoken from between shut teeth, a splash, a scramble, and then I caught sight of the gaunt form of Martin, paddle in hand and hunting-knife between his teeth, loping along toward me, through the tall, rank grass. But, alas! it was too late. The auspicious moment had passed. My fingers one by one loosened their hold, and the deer, gathering all his strength, with a terrific elevation of his hind feet sent me reeling backward, just as Martin, doubled up into a heap, was about to alight upon his back. He missed the back, but, as good luck would have it, even while the buck was in the air,—the deer going up as Martin came down,—the fingers of the guide closed with a full and desperate grip upon his *tail*. Quick as a flash I recovered myself from the bogs, replaced the jack, which fortunately had not been extinguished, upon my head, and stood an interested spectator of the proceedings. Now everybody knows how a wild deer can jump when frightened; and the buck, with Martin fastened to his tail, was thoroughly roused. The first leap straightened the poor fellow out like a lathe, but it did not shake him from his hold. If the reader has ever seen a small boy hanging to the tail-board of a wagon, when the horse was at full speed, he can form a faint idea of Martin's appearance as the deer tore like a whirlwind through the tall grass. Blinded and bewildered by the light, frenzied with fear, the buck, as deer often will, instead of leading off, kept racing up and down, just within the border of light made by the jack, and occasionally making a bolt directly for it. My position was unique. I was the sole spectator of a series of gymnastic evolutions truly original. Small as the audience was, the performers were thoroughly in earnest. Had there been ten thousand spectators, the actors could not have laid themselves out with greater energy. No applause could have got another inch of jump out of the buck, or another inch of horizontal position out of Martin. Whenever, at long intervals, his feet did touch the ground, it was only to leave it for another and a higher aerial plunge. Now and then the buck would take a short stretch into the fog and darkness, only to reappear with the same inevitable attachment of arms and legs streaming behind. The scene was too ludicrous to be endured in silence. The desperate expression of Martin's face, as he was swung round and jerked about, was enough to make a monk explode with laughter while doing penance. I rested my hands on either knee, and laughed until tears rolled down my cheeks. The merriment was all on my side. Martin was silent as death, save when the buck, in some extraordinary and desperate leap, twitched a grunt out of him. Between my paroxysms I exhorted him: it was my time to exhort. "Martin," I shouted, "hang on; that's *your* deer. I quit all claim to him. Hang on, I say. Save his tail anyhow."

Whether Martin appreciated the advice, whether he exactly saw where the "laugh came in," I cannot say, and he could not explain. Still I am led to think that it was to him no trifling affair, but a matter which moved him profoundly. At last the knife was jerked from his teeth, either because of the violence of his exertion, or because he had inadvertently loosened his grasp on it. Be this as it may, Martin's mouth was at last opened, and out of it were projected some of the most extraordinary expressions I ever heard. His sentences were singularly detached. Even his words were widely separated, but brought out with great emphasis. He averaged about one word to a jump. If another got partially out, it was suddenly and ruthlessly snapped off in mid utterance. The result of his efforts to express himself reached my ears very much in this shape: "Jump—*will*—you—be-e—*damned*—I've-e—GOT—you! I'll—hold-d—ON—till—your—ta-i-1—comes—off-f.—*Jump-p-p*—be D-D-DAMNED—I'VE—got—you-u-u."

"Martin," shouted I, "hang on; that's your deer. I quit all claim to him."

When the contest would have ended, what would have been the result had it continued, whether the buck or the guide would have come off the winner, it is not easy to say. Nor is it necessary to speculate, for the close was speedily reached, and in an unlooked-for manner. The deer had led off some dozen jumps out of the circle of light, and I was beginning to think that he had shaken himself loose from his enemy, when all at once he emerged from the fog with Martin still streaming behind him, and made straight for the river. Never did I see a buck vault higher or project himself farther in successive leaps. The Saranacer was too much put to it to articulate a word; only a series of grunts, as he was twitched along, revealed the state of his pent-up feelings. Past me the deer flashed like a feathered shaft, heading directly for the bank. "Hang on, Martin!" I screamed, sobered by the thought that he would save him yet if he could only retain his grip,—"hang to him like death!" He did. Never did my admiration go out more strongly toward a man than it did toward Martin, as, red in the face and unable to relieve himself by a single expression, he went tearing along at a frightful rate in full bolt for the river. Not one man in fifty could have kept his single-handed grip, jerked, at the close of such a struggle as the Saranacer had passed through, and twitched mercilessly as he now was being through the tall bog-grass and over the uneven ground. But the guide's blood was up, and nothing could loosen his clutch. The buck reached the bank, and, gathering himself up for a desperate leap, he flung his body into the air. I saw a pair of widely separated legs swing wildly upward, and the red face of Martin, head downward, and reversed, so as to be turned directly toward me by the summer-sault he was turning, disappeared like a waning rocket in the fog overhanging the river. Once in the water, the buck was no match for his foe. I hurried to the edge of the bank. Beneath me, and half across the river, a desperate struggle was going on. Martin had found his voice, and was using it as if to make up for lost time. In a moment a gurgling sound reached my ears, and I knew that the deer's head was under water; and shortly, in answer to my hail, the guide appeared, dragging the buck behind him. The deer was drowned and quite dead. Drawing my knife across the still warm throat, we bled him well, and, waiting for Martin to rest himself a moment, slid him down into the boat and stretched him at full length along the bottom. Taking our places at either end, and, lift-ing our paddles, we turned our faces campward. Down through the dense, damp fog, cleaving with dripping faces its heavy folds, we passed; glided out of the mist and darkness of the lowland upon the clear waters of the lake, now lively with ripples, and under the brightly shining stars, nor checked our measured stroke until we ran our shell ashore in the glimmer of the fire, by the side of which, rolled in his blanket, with his jacket for his pil-low, John was quietly sleeping. At the touch of the boat on the beach he started up, and the coffee he had made ready to boil at our coming was shortly ready, and, as we drank the warming beverage with laughter which startled the ravens from the pines, and woke the loons, sleeping on the still water of Beaver Bay, we told John the story of our adventure with a buck up Marion River on a foggy night. And often, as I sit in my study, hot and feverish with toil which wearies the brain and wrinkles the face,

I pause, and, throwing down pen and book, fancy myself once more upon that bank, enveloped in fog, with the buck and Martin at his tail, careering before me. Then, with brain relaxed, and eyes which had been hot with the glimmer of the gas on the white sheet cooled and washed in mirthful tears, I turn to pen and book, and graver thoughts, refreshed and strengthened. Blessed be recollection, which, while it allows the ills and cares of life to fade away, enables us to carry all our pleasures and joys forever with us as we journey along!

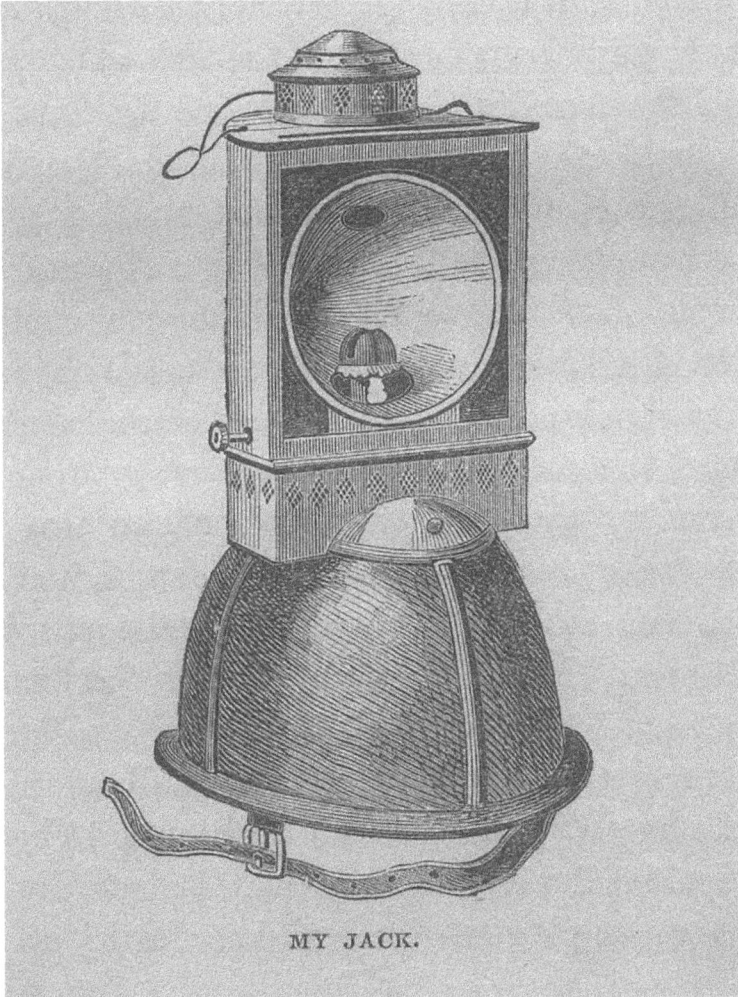

MY JACK.

4

THE STORY THAT THE KEG TOLD ME

Chapter I

THE KEG.

"There is society where none intrudes."

—Byron.

It was near the close of a hot, sultry day in midsummer, which I
had spent in exploring a part of the shore line of the lake where
I was camping, and the tortuous inlet which led into the same;
and wearied with the trip I had made I was returning toward the
camp. There was no motive for haste, and I was taking it easily.
Indeed, I was in that quiet, contented state of mind, into which
one easily falls in the woods, where his labors are dictated by his
amusements and his physical necessities, and not by the duties
which carry with them obligation; and I had done little more than
drift with the lazily-moving current. The quiet inaction, slow as it
was, corresponded with my mood; and I felt almost a regret when
my boat floated out from between the shrubby banks into the open
waters of the little lake.

It was a very secluded sheet of water, hidden away between
the mountains, not marked on the map, and whose existence was
entirely unsuspected by me until in my aimless wanderings I had
a few days before accidentally stumbled upon it. Indeed, I doubt
if in all the woods there is another sheet of water so shut in from
observation and so likely to escape the eye, I will not say of the
tourist and sportsman, but even of the hunter and trapper. It was
because of this fact that I had fallen in love with it. Here was

silence undisturbed by any noise of man's making. Here I could escape the prying eyes of idle and provoking curiosity. Here I could watch the habits of animated nature and study the mystery of her charm without interruption. And here the wisdom which man learns independent of utterance—the wisdom of the unspoken and the unknown—might, so far as I was fit, be received by me.

The first day on the little lake I spent in paddling around its shores, in close scrutiny of them. In every bay into which I successively paddled I expected to find a hunter's cabin. On every point I doubled I looked for a sportsman's lodge. I circled every island in my sharp quest. But in vain. There was not a cabin nor lodge, a charred coal nor mark of a guide's axe or trapper's knife in the entire circuit. Astonished and incredulous, I devoted another day to the examination. I even landed at every spot where Nature had suggested a camp-ground, and searched, with trained eye, for the evidence of man's visitation, but found none; not even the least trace. Springs I found, cool as iced water and clear as crystal; but neither mark of axe, nor knife, nor fire.

Convinced at last, I paddled out to the middle of the lake, feeling, as I watched the sun go down, the shadows deepen and the stars come out, that I beheld what no human eye had ever looked upon: a place unvisited by man from the foundation of the world. In such a place the sense of time passes from you, and the sense of eternity is experienced. The years you have lived, the years of the world, are as if they were not, and you seem to be co-existent with the birth of material things. For are not the mountains around you. as they were when God called them up out of the depths? And is not the sky above them the same? And the great round sun, what has changed it? Yea, and the water, is it not as it was when its parent springs first poured it forth? In such a place one realizes that it is toil and worry and the grief of living, and not years, which make us grow old; for behold, the years rest lightly on whatever is free of these. For that which does not work nor weep is forever young.

And so it came about that the feeling that I was the only man who had ever visited this lake was so forced upon me by what seemed indisputable evidence, that I accepted it as a fixed fact. The idea took utter possession of me, and became a part of my

consciousness. There was not a sign of man nor of man's coming or going, on the shores, and therefore I knew man had never
visited it. To me this was an absolute fact, as sure as life itself.
Well, as I was saying, it was near sunset when my boat drifted on
the current that flowed with easy motion from the little inlet, out
upon the quiet bosom of the lake. The sun was already sinking
in the west, and the peculiar silence which attends the close of a
summer's day in solitary places possessed the atmosphere. The
heat was fast leaving the air and the coolness of the coming night
was growing perceptible to the senses. My camp was only a short
mile down the lake, and toward it, with easy stroke of the paddle,
I urged my homeward course. "To-morrow," I said to myself, as I
paddled along, "I will leave the lake. It is too lonely even for me,
and its steady, unbroken silence day after day is getting oppres-
sive. I am undoubtedly the only man that was ever on this sheet
of water; even the deer here do not know what sort of an animal
I am, and the rats will scarcely get out of the way of my boat. I
will move out of this to-morrow, nor will I stop until I find some
traces of my kind."

Thus muttering to myself I paddled along, watching the reflec-
tions of sky and clouds in the clear unruffled depths beneath, and
thinking of the centuries in which they had received and reflected
back the changes in the firmament suspended above them. I had
already come to the point on the other side of which my camp lay,
when my paddle, as it moved forward for another stroke, struck
against something floating in the water. I might not have noticed
it, perhaps, but for the fact that it sounded hollow as my paddle
struck against it. Curious, because of the peculiarity of the sound,
to know what it was, with a quick turn of my wrist I reversed my
paddle, checked the boat in its course, and with a sharp stroke sent
it backward along the line of its wake. As I repassed the object I
reached down, and finding I could raise it, lifted it into the boat. I
will confess I started as if an electric current had been shot unexpectedly into me. It was a KEG!

Now, finding a keg in some places would not be very surpris-
ing: in a ship yard for instance, or in a cooper's shop or farmer's
cellar, or in a liquor saloon; for in such places kegs are plenty and
you expect to see them. Nor would it have astonished me had I
met it on a frequented river, or in any place where men come and

go; but to find a keg on this lonely lake, where I felt man had never been—where no living soul had ever existed—was, as you will admit, reader, a startling experience. Nevertheless, there it was—a real keg, with oaken staves and iron bands, with a bottom intact, and perfect in all respects save that the head was missing. As I recall it now it is really laughable the way I sat and stared at it. I rubbed my eyes to make sure of my sight. I tapped it with the blade of my paddle and rolled it half over and then back again, to make sure that it was what it seemed.

Convinced at last, I sat and looked at it, questioning. Where did it come from? How did it get there? Who brought it, and when, and for what purpose? Where is he who brought it? Is he living or dead, and where is his camp? These and like interrogations I put to myself as I sat in my boat on that lonely lake, in the growing darkness, looking at that KEG. "Well," I said at last, speaking aloud, as one quickly forms the habit of doing, when alone, "well, sitting here and staring at it don't answer such questions, nor satisfy my hunger, either; and I had better shove in to camp and get supper."

When supper was over and the necessary wood for my fire laid in for the night, I went out for a while, as was my wont, upon the point, for a quiet smoke, and to observe the appearance of the night.

Of the beauty of such a place and hour those who never journeyed beyond the haunts of men know nothing. The sky was without a cloud. The air was breathless. Even the pines had forgotten in slumber their mournful plaint, and stood like so many shadows, dense, motionless and dumb. The water was as moveless as the atmosphere. It received the heaven, as a mirror receives a face. It stole and appropriated the lustre of the firmament, and borrowed from the bespangled sky an ornamentation for its blank spaces as glorious as the heaven's own. The sky was blue-black, and out of its cerulean gloom the pointed stars shot gleams of many-colored fire. The mountains, sombre and vast, rested on their broad bases as if their foundations were laid in everlasting silence. The odors of the forest filled the damp air like incense. A loon far down the lake, as if oppressed by the all-pervading silence, poured into the still air the prolonged sound of its mournful call. It entered into, and lingered sadly for a moment in the air, then passed away, making the silence that followed even more profound. Deeply affected by the spell of the lonely place and the hour, I rose from the stone on which I had been sitting, crossed the point, and returned to my little camp.

I busied myself for a moment or two in starting my fire, and when the flames of it rose clear and strong I seated myself with my back against a pine, and half reclining gazed off upon the lake. As I thus sat watching the reflection of the fire-light in the water, my eyes fell upon the KEG. It seemed, in some sort, a kind of companion to me, alone as I was; a visible bond binding me to my kind; a reminder of the life that men were living in the great, roaring, busy world outside and beyond the lonely lake on whose silent shore I then was lying. It reminded one of life,—or what men call life,—the getting and the giving; the saving and the spending; the loving and the hating; of the thousands far away. I fell again to wondering where it came from, and by whom it was brought over the mountains, and for what purpose;—wondering what its history was, and what had become of him who once handled it;—whether he were living or dead, and a hundred other things such as one might fancy in such a spot, in such an hour, looking at such an object so strangely found. It may be I was awake; it may be I was asleep; but as I was thus looking steadily and curiously at it, and wondering strange things about it, it seemed to change its appearance, and become different from a KEG; even a MAN; a little man; a very little man,—a man not more than eighteen inches high, with the queerest little legs, and the funniest little body, and the tiniest face one ever saw,—but still a *man*. And, then, standing bolt upright and looking straight at me with its little gleaming eyes, that glowed like glistening beads,—wonder of wonders! it opened its diminutive mouth, and began to TALK!

THE STORY OF THE KEG.

"I suppose," it said—and as it began to speak it leaned slightly toward me as a man might in lifting himself upon his toes—and its ludicrous-looking face took to itself a grave expression, funny to see,—"I suppose," it said, "that you are very much astonished to hear me talk, as a man can, and to know that I even have a mouth at all; but I have, sir, a very good mouth indeed, and a tongue inside of it, too, as you will learn before I have done telling my story. For I have seen and heard strange things, both before and since I came into these woods, and had many queer experiences, of which I propose to tell you if you will only sit still and hear me, and not go clean off to sleep as you seem inclined to do. O yes," it continued, "I desire to tell you my story; the story of the man who brought me here; why he did it, and what came of it; and how he lived and died. And it is a very sad story indeed; and it pains me even to recall it." And here the Keg lifted one of its little thin hands, and placed it with great emphasis upon its heart, "but it contains a lesson which it were well that all men, who strive to be rich and are growing to love money, should hear, and I trust that what I tell to you to-night, you will someday tell to them; and I trust it will do them good, and be a warning to them, and make them wiser than was the poor man who once owned me, and who died right here on the point off which you found me,—peace be to his soul! and, indeed, I think he did find peace in the end, although he found it by a weary way, and a steep one, and one which led him nigh into hell. But I will go back to the beginning and tell you all just as it happened, and the reason of things as I saw and felt them long years ago.

IT OPENED ITS DIMINUTIVE MOUTH AND BEGAN TO TALK.   PAGE 13.

"The earliest remembrance I have of myself is of the cooper's shop where I was made; and a nice looking keg I was then, too, although you may not believe it judging by my present appearance. But that was many years ago, and you must remember that years wear the life and beauty out of kegs as much as they do out of men; and although I look so worn and weakly now, yet I can recall the time that my staves were all smooth and clean, so that the oak grain showed clearly from top to bottom of me, and my steel hoops were as bright and shiny as steel can be. I have had many hard knocks since then, and seen hard usage enough to drive the very staves out of me time and again; but the cooper that made me, made me on his honor, and took a deal of honest pride in putting me together, as every workman should in doing his work. And I remember as if it were but yesterday—for I have laughed over it many a time when I had poor reason to laugh at anything—that when I was finished, and the cooper had sanded me off and oiled me so that my side fairly shone, he set me up on his bench and said to his apprentice boy: 'There, that keg will last till the Judgment Day, and well on toward night at that.'"

Chapter II

THE MISER.

"Some lone miser visiting his store
Bends at his treasure, counts, recounts it o'er."
—*Goldsmith.*

"Well, one day, a few weeks after, a man came into the shop and asked the master: 'Have you a good strong keg for sale?' And he put the question in such an earnest, half spiteful and half suspicious way, that I fairly started within my hoops, and opened my eyes wide to take a good look at him; and a very peculiar man I saw, too, I assure you. He was quite a young looking man, not more than forty years of age; of good height and strongly built. He was a gentleman evidently, although his face was darkly tanned and his clothes were old and thread-bare. His mouth was rather small than large. His lips were thin and had a look of being tightly drawn over the teeth—at least it seemed so to me. His chin was very long, and was joined at the base to large, strong jaws. His hair was brownish-black, and not over-abundant; indeed, I am not sure that he had not even then begun to grow slightly bald. But the remarkable feature of his face was his eyes. They were blue-grey in color, smallish in size, and set in deep under the arch of the eyebrows. How hard and steel-like they were, and restless as a rat's! And what an intense look of suspicion there was in them,—a half-scared, defiant look, as if their owner felt every one to be his enemy, against whom he must stand on his guard, and whom he might at any instant have to fight and kill. Ah, what eyes they were! and how they came and went to and from your face, and shot their glances at you and into you—aye, and through you, too. I grew to know them well afterward, and to know what the strange, wild light in them meant; but of that by and by.

"'Have you got a good, strong keg to sell, I say?' he shouted to my master, who was hammering away at a barrel so that he had not heard the man enter, much less his question. 'A good stout keg?' said my master, as he turned around and looked squarely at the questioner. 'I should say that I had, Mr. Roberts; do you want one?' 'Yes,' returned the other, 'I do, but I want a strong one,—*strong*, do you *hear?'*—and he took a step toward my master as if he meant to strike him. 'Strong enough to hold the devil himself if he were in it, or a sinner's hope of heaven, either, if you like that better,' and he sneered the sentence out as if the blessed hope of Paradise were fit only to point a fool's joke. 'Well, I don't know much about the devil, Mr. Roberts,' rejoined my master,—'not so much as you do, it may be; and as to one's hope of heaven, I don't build kegs to keep that in; but there's a keg,'—and my master tapped me with his mallet until I rang clear as a bell—'that I made with my own hands, from the best of stuff, and I said to the boys when I finished it that it would last till the Day of Judgment; and I verily believe it will, if white oak staves and steel hoops can last that long.' 'I didn't ask you anything about the Day of Judgment, or anything else the long-winded parsons talk about and frighten their cowardly followers with,' snarled the other. 'All I want is a good strong keg—strong as can be made of wood and iron—and if that keg is what you say it is, I want it and will take it, if you won't cheat me at the bargain, as I dare say you would like to do; what is your price, eh?' Well, the price was set, the money paid with a muttered protest, and Mr. Roberts hoisted me up under his arm and hastened with me out of the shop.

"Well, you can imagine that I felt very anxious about myself, and wondered as I was being hurried along, where I was being taken, and what use I was to be put to; but I made up my mind to do my duty and hold whatever my new master should give to my trust so that my maker might not hear ill of me; but I little thought what was to befall me, or what I should have to bear as the years went round. For I have seen dreadful sights in my time, and beheld things too awful to declare. For I have seen the undoing of a man, and the wreck of a human soul!

"Well, as I was saying, my new master hurried me along without stopping to speak to any one, although we passed many, and I noticed that no one of all we passed spoke to him, but looked at him coldly or wonderingly, and that he, whenever we were about to meet any one, whether man, woman or child, only clutched me the more tightly and hurried on the faster. At last we came to a common looking sort of a house, set back from the road, with a very high fence built clear around it, and a heavy padlock on the gate, and great, strong, wooden shutters at every window. Into this my master entered and set me down carefully upon the floor. This done, he went back to the door and locked it, and drew two large iron bolts or bars across it, securing them most carefully in the sockets. He then went to every window and examined them to see if each was fastened. He carefully examined every room and closet, even looking into the ash-hole and the oven in the chimney. Then lighting a candle he went down into the cellar, and after that up into the attic, carrying the candle in one hand and a great club or bludgeon in the other.

"By this time I had made up my mind that I had fallen into the hands of a maniac, and that my new master was insane. Leastwise I did not know what to make of him, or what was to be the upshot of his strange ways. After a while he came back to the room where he had left me, and took me up and set me on the table; and starting the upper hoop proceeded to take out one of my heads. At this I was thoroughly frightened, and kept my eyes on him wherever he went, as I wanted to see what his strange conduct meant, and what he would do next. When he had taken one of my heads out, he went to an old drawer under the cupboard and got a large sheepskin, with the wool closely clipped; and with a pair of large shears proceeded to fit me with a lining of it. I must say that he did it with remarkable cleverness, and that when he was done with me I was lined as well as any tailor could line me. But what it all meant I couldn't guess; and so I watched and waited. For you will admit that no keg was ever treated as he was treating me, and that I had good reason to be surprised.

"After he had done lining me with the soft skin he seemed more easy, and less nervous, and he put his hands inside of me and felt of his work and was evidently pleased at it; for he rubbed his hands together, and his eyes glistened, and he said to himself: 'There! I call that a pretty good fit; I don't think old Tim, the tailor, would have done it better.' And then he laughed to himself and rubbed his hands together again as if he had said a very funny thing. By this time it was well on toward night, and he kindled a fire in the fire-place—a very small fire it was, only a little thin blaze made of three or four short sticks which looked as if they had been picked up in the roadway, and a handful or two of chips. But small as the blaze was he managed to heat a little kettle of water by it and cook a cup of tea, which he placed upon an old board-table alongside of a loaf of bread, and then he sat down by the table and began to eat the bread and drink the tea. And this was all the supper he had, and I thought it very strange that so large a man should be content with such a supper; but I grew used to the sight afterward, and ceased to wonder, as you will when you know the cause of his frugality.

After he had done eating, he wrapped the remainder of the bread carefully in a piece of paper, and put it away with the little tea-kettle in the cupboard. And then he went to the door and re-examined the bolts, and looked closely at all the shutters, while I stood and wondered what his strange actions meant, and why he was so anxious that the doors and windows should all be fastened so tightly; for the neighborhood was a good one, and the people law-abiding, so much so that the doors of half the houses in the village were never locked of nights, even from one year's end to another.

When he had done all this, he brought the club or bludgeon that I had seen him carry up stairs with him when he went up into the attic, and laid it on the table beside me, and also a large thick knife, with a strong horn handle, which he had taken from the mantle-piece where it had been lying; and then he went to the ash-hole in the chimney, and brought the ash-pail, which was full of ashes; and he went to the cupboard, and brought an old earthen jar; and from under the bed he fetched a bag; and from a chamber overhead he brought a small box; and from the cellar he returned with a sack, all damp with earth. All the while I kept my eyes well open, you may believe, wondering what it all meant, and what there was in the pail and the jar and the box and the bag and the sack. Well, when he had these all side by side near the table, he sat down and out of the ash-pail he took a small pot, and having blown the ashes off it with great care, he turned it bottom upward oh the table, and—merciful heaven! what do you think was in it?

DOLLARS! GOLD DOLLARS!

Then he took the bag and untied the cord that held the mouth, and emptied it upon the table, and it, too, was full of *dollars*—gold dollars! And then one after the other, he opened the jar and the box and the sack, and out of each and all he poured a great stream of bright golden dollars? Oh, what a pile of them there was! What a heap they made! How they gleamed and glistened! How they jingled and rang! How they rattled and clinked as he poured them down upon the dark boards! And how his eyes gleamed in their deep sockets as they saw the golden stream, and how the thin lips drew apart as the dollars flowed out, until his teeth showed their line of white back of them, and his hands shook and trembled as if the palsy was in them!

It was a dreadful sight to see him sit down, and leaning over the table, run his hands under the yellow heap and lift the pieces up so that the bright bits flowed over and out of his hollow palms and ran down through his parted fingers in shining streams. And then to hear him laugh as he played with the glistening coin! How mirthless his laughter was—hard and sharp and ringing like the metallic ring of the dollars itself. Oh, it was dreadful to think that a human soul could love money so. And he did love it—wildly, madly love it,—love it with all the strength of his strong nature. And this he did not disguise nor deny to himself; but admitted it, and gloried in it, too, with a most wicked and blasphemous glorying, as the Arch Fiend himself is said to glory in his own sin.

He would take a dollar up and look at it as a father might at the face of his favorite child, and pat it with his palm, and smooth the surface of it with a finger tip as if it could feel a caress. Ah me, 'twas dreadful! And then he would take a piece up and talk to it and say, coaxingly, "Thou art better than a wife," and to another, "Thou art sweeter than a child," and to another yet, "Thou art dearer than father or mother." And to the great pile of shining gold, he would say, as he leaned over it, "O my beauties, the parsons may say what they please, but you are better than a far-off heaven." Ah, such blasphemy as I heard that night! How the sweet and blessed things of human life were derided, and the things that are divine and holy sneered at!

At last he fell to counting them, and by the way he did it I knew he had done it often; done it so many times that he counted as men do things by habit,—mechanically. He would say: "ONE, TWO, THREE, FOUR, FIVE, SIX, SEVEN, EIGHT, NINE, TEN,—GOOD! ONE, TWO, THREE, FOUR, FIVE, SIX, SEVEN, EIGHT, NINE, TEN— GOOD!" And so go on, faster and faster, until his breath was gone; and then he would catch it again, and start anew. "ONE, TWO, THREE, FOUR, FIVE, SIX, SEVEN, EIGHT, NINE, TEN,—GOOD!" Oh, it was awful to think of an immortal being loving MONEY so!

For a long time he counted on; counted until his hands shook, and the sweat stood thick on his forehead, and his eyes gleamed and glowed as if he were mad. And perhaps he was mad,—as all men are who live for gain, and whose hearts are fired with the awful lust for gold. So he counted on. And when he had counted all,—even to the very last,—the old dark boarded table was covered thick with little piles of tens; and he arose with a jump like a maniac, and stood above the table and shouted until the old house rang again:

"SIXTEEN THOUSAND, SIX HUNDRED AND SIXTY-SIX DOLLARS! SIXTEEN THOUSAND, SIX HUNDRED AND SIXTY-SIX DOLLARS!"

Well, after a while he sobered down and became quiet, and began to pick the dollars up and pack them away inside of me,—carefully, one by one, as a mother might lay her children in their beds to sleep,—and this he kept on doing until the last shining coin had been taken from the table, and I was full to the very brim. Then he put my head in its place, and drove the upper hoop on snug, and put me in the bed, and the great knife under his pillow; and, blowing out the light, lay down beside me and putting one arm across me as if I were a child, fell asleep. And over the old house in which the miser lay clasping me to his heart, I knew the stars were shining; and beyond the stars, with eyes that never slept, I knew that the great God was looking down upon him and me.

Chapter III

THE MISER'S FEAR.

"I greatly fear my money is not safe."

—*Shakespeare.*

"Increase his riches and his peace destroy,
Now fears in dire vicissitude invade,
The rustling brake alarms, and quivering shade,
Nor light nor darkness brings his pain relief;
One shows the plunder and one hides the thief."

—*Johnson.*

Well, things went on in the same fashion day after day, and night after night; but getting worse all the time. My master did little work, and of course earned little money,—only enough to buy his bread and tea, with now and then a little piece of meat. He seemed to have no desire to get more, but was only anxious to keep what he had. And about this he was so anxious that it kept him in a fever of excitement all the time. For days he would scarcely go beyond the doorway, and if he saw a man coming along the road he would come in with great haste, close the shutters and bar the door as if he feared the man was a robber and was coming to rob him. And indeed this was his feeling. He was never for an instant free of the fear of losing his money. He would mutter about it in the day time, and he would mutter about it in the night when he was asleep. Many a time have I heard him, in the dead of the night when the old house was as still as a tomb, suddenly break out and say, "Oh, you don't want my money, eh? You came for it, you know you did, and you hope by crying to get it out of me; but you shan't have a dollar of it; no not a dollar! D'ye hear?—if it would save your soul!" And then he would put out his arms and wrap them around me and strain me to him, muttering and murmuring about his "Beautiful dollars. My own, own DOLLARS, they want to get you from me. I know them; but they shall never do it, for I would kill them if they tried." And he would grind and grit his teeth and hoarsely repeat the word, *"kill,—kill,"* as he sunk again into a heavy sleep.

It was bad enough to hear his muttering when all was quiet and peaceful, and his sleep was undisturbed; but when the night was stormy and wild, and the wind made the old house shake, and the rain was slashed in great sheets against the windows, and the timbers in the framework creaked and groaned;—at such times, he would toss and moan in his bed, shriek and clutch me with his fingers, leap up and strain and tug and strike as if he were wrestling with an unseen person, who was striving to carry me away. Indeed, waking or sleeping, he was tormented with a deadly fear; and the fear was born of the suspicion that some one would succeed in stealing me, and the treasure in me.

And this suspicion it was that had poisoned his whole life, and made him hate his kind, and driven him into the wretched strait he was in, when I came to him. And a more wretched strait no mortal was ever in; for what is worse than the suspecting of one's kind, even of one's wife and child; yea, and of the man of God himself, whose love for you is as God's,—the deep, steady, ministering love of the soul. And this was just his case, as I found out one day. And this was the way it came about:—

It was summer; and for the sake of comfort—for the old house was damp and close—he had left the door wide open, and, seating himself in his chair, had fallen asleep. Indeed, I was rather drowsy myself, and was fast dropping off into a nap, when I heard my master give a horrible yell, and leap with a frightful oath to his feet. My eyes, as you can imagine, came open with a snap; and the sight I beheld nearly upset me. In the doorway stood a man and woman; and by his dress I knew the man to be the old village pastor, and the woman I soon learned was my master's wife. For a minute my master stood looking at them, and then he said abruptly, "What in the Devil's name did you come here for?"

"John," said the woman, "your child, Mary, is dying; and I thought you, who are her father, might want to see her before she passed away"; and her voice choked, and I saw her breast under her dress heave with suppressed sobs.

"Dying, is she?" said my master brutally. "I don't believe it: it's a trumped-up story of yours to get me away from here, that you may steal my gold; but you can't fool me with your lying, and you might as well get away from here, both of you."

"John," returned the woman,—and as she spoke the great tears came into her eyes, and her hands twitched convulsively,—"John, I never lied to you, nor to any one, in my life, and you know it. Mary is dying, as the parson here can tell you; and I dare not let her die, and not give you a chance to see her; for she was the last one born to us, and you did love her before the cursed love of gold in you drove from your heart all other loving. And I said the father should see the child before she dies: it is his right; and so I have come and told you. And besides, Mary herself last night spoke your name in her sleep, and talked in her wanderings of you; and this morning she said suddenly, 'I wish I could see father before I die. I dreamed of him last night: it was an awful dream; and I wish I might tell it to him before I go. It might be it would do him good, and win his heart from his dreadful gold.' And so, John, I got this man of God to come along with me, that he might bear witness to my truth, and perhaps speak a word of wisdom to you."

While the woman had been speaking, my master had stood looking at her with the same scowl on his face, and the same hard, suspicious expression in his eyes. Not a muscle changed, nor a line softened. So he stood a moment, glaring at them; and then he said to the minister, who was leaning on his cane,—for he was old and weak, and his head was white as snow,—"Well, what have you got to say?"

"John Roberts," said the old man solemnly, "I have much to say; for I bring a message, not from your dying child, but from your living Lord. I remember when I baptized you as a child at the altar, on the day your pious parents gave you in holy covenant to God. And I remember when I married you to this woman here, your wife; and I remember your early promise, and the happiness you had yourself and made for others, until the lust of gold possessed you. And I have known your downward path, and how that which God meant for good, became by your perversion of its use, an evil to you,—yea, an evil which poisoned all your life, and changed the course of it; turned you against your friends, made you brutal to your wife and child, and brought you to the gate of hell, where you now stand,—a miserable miser! All this I have watched and seen and known; and all this I have warned you against time and again in past years, and in the name of Him who was sold to death by a miser like yourself. And now I call upon you to repent, and by true repentance and deep contrition find mercy in Him whom you have sold out of your heart and life, and in whose eyes you are another Judas, yet lacking repentance. Repent, therefore, and return to your right mind, lest a worse thing fall upon you, and the curse of your life be doubled upon you in your death, even that as you are now deserted of man you may in that dreadful hour find yourself deserted of God. And as for your child, as your wife has said, she is dying, and she has asked for you. She bids you come to her before she dies. For God has spoken to her in a vision, as he did to some of old, and revealed to her what shall be if you repent not,—a dreadful death, in a wild spot, with no one nigh, and a darkness round about you in your death-hour like the darkness that surrounds the damned,—all this she has seen with eyes prepared by the mystery of the Unknown to see it; and I pray you, therefore, as one standing between the living and the dead, that you come right speedily and see your child, and hear her message, lest she die, and leave it unspoken, and what she has seen in vision be realized in fact, and you be lost in death even as you are already lost in life."

He paused, and his face shone as one who speaks beyond the measure of the spirit of man—even by the measure of the Spirit of God,—and his aged hands shook; and when he had ended, his lips continued to move, as with one who follows an exhortation with an inaudible prayer.

But my master remained unmoved. He heard the words of his old Pastor, as he had the words of his wife, with the same scowling, sinister look in his eyes; the same set, doggedness of face, the same sneering expression on his lips. He stared at them a moment, and then shouted: "You LIE! both of you,—you want my money, you mean to steal it from me. Everybody wants it; there isn't an honest man in the world. All are thieves. All love gold. You do. I know by your looks you love it. You can't fool me by your tears and your preaching. You get out of this house or I will kill you," and he swore a horrible oath, and stepping back a step he seized the bludgeon and swung it round his head, and stamped his foot upon the floor and swore at them again; his eyes glowed like hot coals, and the froth hung on his lips. The woman ran screaming from the house, but the old pastor stood his ground, and faced him, and said:—

"John Roberts, thou art a doomed man. Thou hast denied the truth and resisted the Spirit, and Satan hath thee in full possession. The lust of gold that destroys many is in thee strong and mighty, and only God can save thee, nor he against thy will. Repent, or thou shalt perish in a lonely spot, on a dark night, with none to help nor hear thy cries; and thy gold shall perish with thee." And so saying, he turned and slowly left the house.

For a moment my master stood, and then he rushed for the door and locked it, and slid the great strong bars into their sockets; and then he came and lifted me upon the table, and patted me with his hand, and laughed and said: "My gold! my gold!" And when night came he took my head out and poured the shining pieces upon the table, and played with them for hours, and then, as was his fashion, he fell to counting them by tens in the same manner as was his custom, saying: "ONE, TWO, THREE, FOUR, FIVE, SIX, SEVEN, EIGHT, NINE, TEN. GOOD!" until he had counted them to the very last one. As he counted the frenzy grew on him, and when his task was over, and the old dark-wood table was all yellow with the gold pieces lying in stacks of ten, he was wild in the joy of his terrible lust. He leaped and danced around the glistening coins, and shouted till the old house rang: "SIXTEEN THOUSAND SIX HUNDRED AND SIXTY-SIX!"

And then he put them all back within me, fastened my head in tightly, laid me in his bed, laid himself beside me, and, putting an arm around me, he fell asleep. And I knew that over the old house the stars were shining brightly, and that above the stars the Great God, with eyes that never slept, was looking calmly down on him and me.

But when he woke in the morning he was not as he had been, but more nervous and savage-like. He did not unbar the door during the whole day, nor open the heavy shutters an inch, but kept all closed and dark. And he was muttering and talking to himself all day. He had the look of one who was planning some deep plot, nor could I make out what it was; but I caught enough of his talk to know that he was more suspicious of losing his money than ever, and trusted no one, but was afraid of all men, known and unknown, and was thinking and planning how to make his money safe and get me to some spot where no one could steal me. Once I heard him say: "All men are thieves. I suspect them all. No one with money is safe among them. They will get it yet, unless I go where they cannot find me." And then he would curse his kind and swear.

At last he suddenly stopped in his tramping up and down the room, and shouted: "I'll *go*, go where they cannot find me. Go where I can be alone and can count my money as much as I wish, in the broad day, under the bright sun or stars, and see it glint and glisten in the bright light. Won't that be glorious!—to be alone with my money, where I can spread it all out in broad day and see it shine, and count it over and play with it, with no one nigh to scare me nor make me hide it away, for fear of its being seen and stolen. Men, curse them, are what I dread. I will go where there is not a man!"

Chapter IV

THE MISER IN THE WOODS.

"Gold, gold, gold, gold,
Bright and yellow hard and cold."

—Hood.

After this he said no more, but packed up the few things he had, and rolled me up in a blanket and put me in a sack, so I could neither see nor hear a single thing that was done or said, and that is all I know of what happened for many a day, only I knew by my feeling that I was being *carried*, CARRIED, CARRIED, over rivers and mountains, and through forests that were wide and deep, until one day I felt myself put in a boat; and on we went, day after day, night after night, until one afternoon, I knew not when, neither the year nor the day, the boat stopped, the bag in which I was, was carried ashore, and, for the first time for many a day, I was taken out of it, and I saw the sunlight once more, and behold! I was on the very point off which you this evening found me."

And here the keg paused a moment, as one who is tired of rapid talking, or oppressed by mournful memories; and it made a motion as if it would sit down, but did not. But it put one little hand up to its chin and rested for a moment so, and I thought it fetched a little sigh, but of that I am not sure, for it might have been a puff of wind playing with the uppermost tuft of some neighboring pine, or the sputtering of the lire, for that matter; but in a moment it began again.

"You must pardon my stopping a moment, but I have not done much talking for many a year and it really takes the breath out of me; moreover one of my heads is gone, and that makes a great difference with a keg I assure you; for we are like a great many men who manage to get along with one head, but no one sees how they do it, and all heartily wish they had another in addition to the one they have, and a better one too. And besides I am getting rather old, and I doubt if I live much longer, for ever since I have been standing here, by the fire, I have felt that I might fall to pieces at any moment," and the keg cast an anxious look down over itself and then as if partially strengthened, at least, went on:—

"Well, things continued very much as they were at the old house for several weeks, and my master seemed happy in the thought that he had got beyond the reach of men and the danger of their stealing me, and what I had in me. Every day when the sun shone brightly he would take me down to the point yonder, from beneath the shadow of the pines, where the sun shines clearly, and pour the treasure out in one great pile and play with it by the hour. It seemed to please him greatly to see the yellow coins shine and shimmer in the bright light, and he would lie in the sand and watch the sparkling heap by the hour, and count it all over and over again, and laugh and shout while doing it as he used to do around the old table when we were in the house. And it seemed more dreadful to me than ever before, for here everything was so still and solemn, and the sky seemed so grave, the sun so strong and bright, and the mountains so vast and majestic, and all things so suggestive of God and Eternity, that it seemed blasphemy for a human being to be thinking so much of his money. Indeed, the sky and water and mountains, and even the trees, seemed to have eyes and to be looking straight down at him as he sat there in the sand counting his money, as if wondering what use it could all be to him.

But after a time I could see that a change was coming over my master. He grew grave and quiet, and moved about in a noiseless way, very unlike his old fashion of acting and talking. So, gradually, a change came over him until he was not at all as he had been. He left off counting his money for days at a time, and when he did count it, it was in a listless manner, just the reverse of his old-time fashion. He would even go away and leave the yellow heap on the sand unwatched, and uncared for, while he sat looking at the shadow of the mountain in the water, or lay stretched at full length on his back, a stone for his pillow, his hands crossed on his breast and his eyes gazing fixedly up at the heavens. You may imagine that I was very much puzzled at all this, and wondered what it all meant, for I could see that something was preying on his mind, and that a great change was coming over him.

"AND COUNT IT ALL OVER AND OVER AGAIN." Page 34.

One day he came, and packing the gold within me, put the head in with the greatest care; and when it was done he stood looking at me a moment and then said, "I think I will never open you again," and he said it in such a sad sort of a way that I was vastly puzzled.

Indeed, I did not believe him, but fancied that he was not feeling over-well, and was low spirited like because of it, and that when he came to himself he would come around and count what was in me as happily as ever. But a greater surprise was in store for me; for when he went to the camp, which was in this very place you have here to-night, he did not take me with him, but left me there alone on the beach. I did not think much of it at first, for I said to myself, he will be back by and by and carry me in with him to the camp as he always does; but the minutes passed and kept passing and still he did not come, and at last I gave him up and decided that I must pass the night where I was, alone. Well, as you can fancy, I felt very strangely in view of it, and rather nervously, too, for I had never spent a night alone by myself since my master owned me, nor outside a house or tent either, for that matter; so as I have said I felt a little nervous about it. But I made up my mind to be as brave as I might and put as good a face on the matter as I could. But it was a very strange experience I had that night, and one I have never forgotten. You see it was the first night I ever spent alone in the wilderness, and it made an impression on me I shall never forget, and although I have passed many nights since alone in this solitary spot, yet never has there been one to me like that first one. The shadows of the mountains were so dark and heavy that they appeared to burden the lake as with a ponderous bulk, and the very water that reflected their vast sides seemed oppressed by their presence. The sky was blue-black; a grave and sombre sky it was. In it only a few stars shone, and those with shortened beams. The silence was like an atmosphere. It rested upon the mountains, brooded on the water, and slept amid the shadows of the still trees. And yet, dark as it was, I felt that in it was an eye, and, silent as it was, I felt that out of it would come a voice—an Eye that looked in steady but unwrathful condemnation upon me, and a Voice that spoke in solemn judgment, although with inaudible tones.

It seemed as if the sin of my master was being charged upon me, and that the whole universe was visiting upon me its contempt. O! sir, I saw strange sights that night, and heard sounds that made me shrink within my hoops in fear. Bands of angels all robed in white, and flying on white wings, came and stood poised in the air above me, and pointed at me with their white hands, and as they gazed, their sweet faces dilated with horror. Devils, too, great black beings and shapes that were shapeless, whose faces were those of hell, and eyes bloodshot with torture, came, and poising above me, would point with their black fingers insultingly downward; and laugh with horrid mirth; then sail away until their black wings faded in the farther gloom. And I heard moans in the air as of a woman moaning for bread; and prayers as of a dying child, dying with a dread at her heart for someone whose sin lay on her soul; and sounds as of many noises mixed in one: prayers and curses, oaths and snatches of hymns. And out of the stillness of the outward space—the stillness of the far-off and the far-up and the beyond, I seemed to hear a great voice continually saying; "THE MAN THAT LOVETH MONEY OVERMUCH IS DOOMED. THE MAN THAT LOVETH MONEY OVERMUCH IS DOOMED."

"At last the sun rose, and right glad was I to see it, but little did I dream when I saw it come up over the mountain yonder, what would happen before it rose again. For of all days in my life that was the most eventful, and I do not expect you to believe me when I tell you what took place in it; but I shall tell you the truth, nevertheless, and of things just as they happened.

About ten o'clock in the morning my master came to the point where I was, and his face was as I had never seen it before. It was the face of a man who had suffered much, and was suffering. His hair lay matted on his damp forehead; his eyes were blood-shot; his teeth set, and his mouth white at the corners, while his hands were clinched as the hands of one in a spasm. He came and stood directly over me, and in a voice hard and strained said:—

"For thee, thou cursed gold, I have wasted my life and ruined my soul."

This he said many times. Then he walked away and stood and talked to himself; and I heard him say: "*He* said, 'Unless you repent, you shall die on a dark night, in a lonely spot, with no one nigh.'" And he kept repeating, "On a dark night, in a lonely spot, with no one nigh." And then he would look around him at the trees and the mountains and the solitary shores.

After a while he began to walk up and down the point, and wring his hands and smite them on his breast, and cry out: "Oh! if I COULD do it! Oh! If I COULD do it! Perhaps there would be hope for me: perhaps there would be hope for ME!" And me would emphasize the ME in such a plaintive, pitiful tone as was never done, I think, by man before. Once he got down on his knees, and clasped his hands together, and I wondered what he was going to do, for I had never seen a man in that position before, and it looked so queer; but in an instant he leaped to his feet and cried: "NO, NO! It is no use. Forgiveness is not for me: forgiveness is not for me."

And so the day passed, and a fine day it was, too, for though my master was in such trouble, and the grip of a dire distress was on him, yet the sun took no note of it, but shone as brightly in the sky, and the trees swung as merrily to and fro as the breeze blew through them, and the ripples ran laughing along the curved beach as if there were never such a thing as human trouble in the world.

Toward night, just before the sun went down, my master came, and taking my head out, stood for a while looking at the gold within me; then he said slowly to himself: "Perhaps I may have strength to do it: perhaps I may have strength to do it." And then he sat down on the sand and gazed far off, as one whose thoughts are not in his eyes. And there in the one spot, without moving, he sat, while the sun went down, the shadows of evening settled slowly and darkly on shore and lake and mountain range, until at last night like a mantle lay darkly on the world. There, in the stillness, my master sat, his face hidden by the gloom, thinking—I knew not what. At last he moved; and, as if too weak to rise, crawled along on the sand to my side, and steadying himself on his knees, he placed his hands together, and lifting his face to the dark blue heaven above, found speech, and began to talk to One I could not see:—

"O Thou, who art the Lord of this great world; whose eyes see every creature thou hast made; and whose ear is open to their cry, see me to-night, and hear my prayer. Bound have I been, and bound I am, to sin. My soul, pursued by evil, knows not where to flee. My life has been a hell, and out of hell I seek deliverance here and now. Come to my aid or I am lost! Save me in mercy or I am doomed! Give thou me strength, for I am weak, and may not do what I would do, without thy aid. Out of this stillness speak to me. Here where no man may hear, hear thou my cry. Thou Lord of heavenly mercy, lend me thine aid!"

He paused, and rising to his feet, lifted me, and started toward the bushes where he kept his boat, and placing me in it shoved out upon the lake, and paddled toward the center, saying slowly and solemnly to himself: "Lend me thine aid, O Lord! Lend me thine aid!" At last we reached the center of the lake, and having checked the boat, he sat for a moment without saying a word; then lifting his face upward he said in a low, sweet voice: "Dear Lord, thou hast given of thy strength. I thank thee,"—then raised me in his arms and———"

A rattle and a crash, as of pieces of wood lading suddenly in a heap, and my eyes came open with a snap. My fire had smouldered down, and a thin column of blue smoke was rising, unattended by flame, in a wavy spiral through the air. The moon had found an opening in the pines overhead, and was pouring its white beams upon the whiter ashes. The keg I had picked from the lake, heated by the fire, had shrunken in its staves until the rusty iron bands afforded them no support; and shaken by the slight jar of a crumbling brand, or falling pine-cone, perhaps, had tumbled inward and lay in a confused heap. I rubbed my eyes, stretched out my chilled legs, and said to myself: "What a queer dream! I really thought that keg was talking to me. If it had kept on much longer it would have persuaded me that the old fellow, its master, or his ghost, is actually on this lake now. Egad! I think it would start even my pulse a little to see a man in a boat on this lake to-night."

Half laughing to myself at the silly suggestion that my fancy had made, I rose to my feet, stretched myself, yawned, and stepping down to the edge of the water looked off upon the lake. I am not ashamed to say that I started, and the blood chilled a little in my veins at what I saw. There, off the point, *within twenty feet of where I found the keg, was a boat and a man sitting in it—motionless as if carved from the air!*

Chapter V

JOHN NORTON THE TRAPPER.

"Nature's Nobleman."

—Thompson.

Well, I will admit that I was surprised, greatly surprised, for I knew that there was not a living being on that lake at sunset—nor had there been for days, or years for that matter: for there is no place in all the world, save cities, where man can go and stay even a night and not leave marks of his presence, and on all this lake shore there was not a trace of any human being. Yet in spite of all this evidence forbidding the supposition, there sat a man, paddle in hand, in a boat, not forty rods from where I stood. I knew that I was well concealed from view, for the shadows in which I stood was as dark as the matted branches of the rich cedars that lined the lake-shore and projected outward over the water, could make it; and so I kept my station without moving an inch, and watched.

For a full minute the boat lay on the level water as if it had grown up out of it, and was a part of the lake itself, so steadfastly did it hold its place and I could well guess what was passing in the mind of him whose form was as motionless as the boat, but whose eyes I knew were searching every inch of the shore line, and whose thoughts were as busy as his eyes. He had evidently come round the point as little expecting the presence of man as I had anticipated his, and some flitting spark, or the gleam of some coal,—or likelier yet the thin filament of blue smoke rising from the smouldering and ash-covered embers,—had caught his eye and brought his boat to a stand as quickly as a reversed paddle could do it. In a moment the boat began to move; so slowly, so easily, so steadily, that the eye could scarcely detect the movement. I laughed silently to myself to see the familiar motion of ambushing a camp from the water side, done so skilfully. For whoever he was, or whatever his errand, the man in that boat knew how to handle a paddle as only a few ever learn the art,—to perfection. His body never moved. The bent posture of it never changed. His head kept its fixed position. The arms worked from the shoulder-sockets, and were lifted with a movement so slow and gradual that the eye that could measure their extension and return must needs be keen of sight, nor lose its observation by a wink. The boat did not start—it simply ceased to stand still; but that fraction of an instant at which it ceased to stand still and began to move, no human eye could tell. Slowly, slowly, so slowly that at times I doubted if it did move at all, the boat came floating on. For ten minutes had it been moving, and yet it had barely covered as many rods. Then the motion of the arms died out in the air, and the boat again stood still. But the body of the boatman still kept its fixed position, and the arms still hung suspended in the atmosphere, where they were when the will of the paddler had checked them.

"By Jove!" I said to myself, "that man acts as if he wants to murder some one, or fears someone will murder him: but he understands how to do a job like the one he is at, and I would like to know how long it has taken him to learn that use of the paddle."

A few minutes passed, then the arms began to rise and fall again, and the boat stole slowly into motion. Again ten rods were covered; again the little boat came to a pause. It was now barely fifty yards away, and the full moon made it an easy matter to study quite closely both the boat and boatman. The boat was of the common build, sharp at either end, low-sided and light. In the bow was a pack-basket, while a hound lay crouched in the middle. A rifle was resting across the paddler's knees. Of his face I could discern little, because the moon was at his back. In a moment he laid the paddle softly across the boat; lifted his rifle as noiselessly from his knees, and rose slowly to his feet. All this had been done as only a skilled boatman and woodman could do it: not a jerk nor awkward motion in the process, but coolly, deliberately, and without the least suggestion of a sound.

"Few men could have lifted themselves from their seat in a boat like that in the style he has done it," I said to myself, "and few dogs would lie as that dog lies, in a boat maneuvered as that has been for the past twenty minutes, without stirring nose or foot. I wonder he has not scented me."

That very instant, even as the thought was passing in my mind, my ear caught the sound of the lowest possible whine from the hound; but his body never stirred, and his nose, active as it must have been, never lifted itself a baud's width from its resting place on the bottom of the boat.

"Hollo, the camp there!" said the man in the boat suddenly. "Be ye sleeping or dead, man or ghost, whom I find in this lonely spot to-night?"

"Not dead, nor asleep," said I, speaking from the dense gloom of the overhanging cedar; "but wide awake and watchful as it behooves a man to be, in a place like this, with a man ambushing his camp in the dead of night. Put down your rifle and come into camp if you want to. The sound of a human voice coming out of your throat makes me feel friendly, whoever you are. Come in, and I will stir up the fire and we can see how we like each other's looks."

So saying, I stepped back to where my wood was piled, and proceeded to thrust a dozen pitchy knots and a huge roll of white birch-bark into the embers. The few remaining coals beneath the ashes caught eagerly at the pitch thus thrust against them, and after an instant's sputtering the inflammable material leaped suddenly into a roaring flame. As the blaze shot upward, I rose from my knees on which I had dropped to give the embers an encouraging puff, and the man, leaning on his paddle-staff, with the hound crouched at his feet, stood before me.

For a moment we stood and looked at each other, as two men might, meeting for the first time, at such an hour, in such a place,—looked each other over thoroughly, from head to foot, and then satisfied, at least on my part, I said:—

"Old man, you are welcome."

"Thank ye; thank ye," replied my visitor. "I shouldn't have dropped in upon ye in this onseemly way, and at sech an onseemly hour, but the line of yer smoke took me onawares like as I turned the pint yender, for I didn't expect to find a human bein' on these shores, and I half doubted if a mortal man was here, till my hound got yer scent in his nose and signalled me that flesh and blood was nigh. And so I ax yer pardin for comin' in on ye as I did, more like a thief than an honest man; but I have memories of this spot that made me think strange things, and fear that all was not right. Young man, what may yer name be?"

"I am called, when at home, Henry Herbert," I said, "but you can split it in the middle if it would fit your mouth better in that way, and take it half at a time, and call me Henry or Herbert as you please; for I know one about as well as I do the other, and answer to either pretty readily; and since you are getting on in years, and are old enough to be my father, with a good liberal margin at that, you had better take the first half of it; and so, if you please, you may call me Henry for short."

"Well, Henry," said the old man, and there came a beaming look of good nature into his eyes as he spoke, with the least twinkle of humor playing in and penetrating the benevolence of it, "I *am* gittin pritty well on in years, and ye don't seem much more than a youngster to me, although ye have managed to git a pritty good growth in the time ye have been at it; and perhaps the comin' and goin' of years has put some things inside my head that boys can't be expected to git, while they have been whitenin' the outside of it; so, mayhaps, it is well enough that I should call ye by yer Christian name, as if I was yer own father; although I have never had a boy of my own, or a wife or home either, for that matter; onless ye can call these woods a home; for I have seen sixty year come and go sence I came into them, and the Lord has cared for me in summer's heat and winter's cold through them all,—so well that I haven't had a wish for other company than I have found with the animils and things He has made, or for any other home than He has builded for me by His own hands." And the old man paused a moment, and looked lovingly down at the hound which lay stretched at his feet, with his muzzle resting on his paws, as if, in the dog, I could see one of the companions which had supplied with affection a heart that had missed the love of wife and children.

"Yis," he continued, "the woods have been a home for me for the number of years that measure the life of mortal man, and there is leetle in them I haven't seen, and few are the noises that natur' makes that my ears haven't heerd; and I know all their paths and their ways as well as a man in the settlements knows his door-yard. But that ain't neither here nor there,"—as if he was conscious of having fallen into a musing mood, and would check himself—"that's neither here nor there," he continued, "and I am glad to have run agin ye here to-night, although the seemin' of things was agin me. For I did ambush yer camp as a thief of a half-breed might; but I was taken onawares by yer camp smoke, and startled, as ye would well understand to be reasonable in me, did ye know what I know of this spot, and the strange goin's on that has been here years agone, as I know them; and it seems queer to me to find a livin' bein' to-night, where I thought there was only a dead man's grave. But I am glad to have run agin ye, Henry Herbert, for I have heerd of ye many times in the last ten years, as one who loved the woods and the way men live in them, and knowed the proper use of a rifle, and how to handle the paddle as some born to the use of it never larn it; and I have heerd that yer eye was keen and finger sure, as a hunter's should be, and that ye let no buck run off with yer lead, but dropped him dead in his tracks where he stood—which is marciful and decent in a man who handles a rifle. And I have heerd, mor'over, that ye loved to be alone, and to find things out that natur' never tells to a company; and that ye boated up and down through the woods all by yerself, sleepin' where night overtook ye like an honest man, and I know'd that I should some day cross yer trail and jine ye; but I leetle thought to run agin' ye here to-night, for I'd no idee that mortal man know'd this lake, save me and him whose body I buried here eleven years gone this fall." And the old man paused, seated himself on the butt of a log, and gazed with a solemn look in his face into the fire.

I did not feel quite like breaking in on his meditations, whatever they might be; and so I stood and looked at him. In a few moments he began:—

"I ax yer pardin if it be axin' too much of ye, but I've fetched my boat through fifty miles today, and it's nigh on twenty hours sence I've tasted food: not but that I could have had enough—for I run agin a buck on Salmon Lake this arternoon jest as the sun was goin' down, that was big enough to keep a Dutch parson in venison for a week, and that sizes him pritty big, as ye know, if ye ever camped with one of 'em"—and the old man opened his mouth and laughed a peculiar, good-natured laugh, that showed more on the face than it gave forth noise—"but I was in a hurry to git through here and couldn't stop to dry him, and I never settle lead into any cretur I can't use for meat, unless it be a fur-bearin' animil or a wicked panther. So I jest paddled up to him ontil I could flirt some water onto his shoulders, and I landed about two quarts on his back, and the way the cretur jumped sot my eyes swimmin'." And here the old man laughed again in his own peculiar fashion. "But, as I was sayin', I haven't tasted food sence the last day dawn, and feel sort of empty like; and somehow latterly the night mists seem to git into me more'n they used to when I was younger, for age thins the blood, and cools it, too, for that matter; an' if ye feel like botherin' yerself that much ye may cook me a pot of tea and give me a cold cake, if one be lyin' round; and if ye happen to have a bit of buck ye fear won't keep till mornin' I guess I could keep it for ye in a spot where I've put a good deal of that kind of meat in the last sixty year;" and the old man laughed again, in his hearty, noiseless manner, as if greatly pleased at his own homely and innocent wit.

"Old man," said I, "you just sit on that log a few minutes, and I will give you a drink of tea that will warm your blood as if forty years had been taken from your record; and as for cold cakes, I don't keep that article, but here is some batter"—and I uncovered a pan standing a little back from the fire—"that will make cakes so light that you will have to hold them down with your fork; and look at that"—and I swung out of my birch bark cupboard a roll of tenderloin steak twelve or fourteen inches long—"I'll spit that for you so that it will dissolve in your mouth, and go down your throat like honey; and you and I will have a feast that will make us feel as full as a doe in the lily-pads,—for I know whom I have for my guest to-night as well as if you had told me your name, and right glad am I to have the best shot that ever drew bead, and the best boatman that ever feathered a paddle, and as honest a guide as ever drew breath, in my camp, and there's my hand, and you are welcome to all I have in my pack, and to all I can do for you, John Norton"—and I stretched my hand out to the old man, who met its palm with his own in a hearty, hunter-like grip.

"Well, well," laughed the old man, as he re-seated himself on the log, while I bestirred myself with preparations for the meal, "I sorter suspicioned that ye knowed who I was, but I didn't know for sartin; for ye carry a mighty steady face, and ye didn't let on with yer eyes what ye was thinkin' about, as most youngsters do; but I take yer welcome in the same way ye give it, and if old John Norton can do anything to make yer stay in the woods more pleasant-like to ye, or larn ye any trick of beast or bird, or tell ye anything of natur's ways that ye haven't larnt as yit—ye may

depend on it, young man, that he will larn it to ye;"—and so saying he relapsed into silence, but watched me steadily as I kept on
with my work.

In a few minutes the bark that served for a table was put in front
of him, with the plates and cups, the pepper, salt, sugar, and such
other luxuries as my pack afforded, and I poured the old man a
cup of the best that ever came from Formosa, while I kept on turning the cakes and the steak.

"Well, now, that's the best tea I ever tasted, for sartin," said the
old man, as he sipped the stimulating beverage—"it's as smooth
as spring water, and goes down a man's throat as easy as an otter
goes into a crick. I never tasted drink that the Lord hadn't made,
for sixty year of my life, but latterly, 'specially at night, or when
over-tired, it does seem to me that a few leaves of tea, judiciously
steeped as ye have done it, sort of strengthens the water and makes
a kind of improvement on the Lord's own work, if it be right for a
mortal to say so; leastwise," he added, as he took a deeper quaff,
"this is mighty pleasant warmin' to the ribs, and sort of makes a
man feel inhabited-like inside, and not empty as a shanty with
nobody in it;" and the look of placid contentment that came to the
old man's face was a picture to see.

By this time, the meal was ready, and we sat down on either
side of the bark table, in the glow of the fire-light, to eat.

"Henry," said the old man, as he drew his hunting knife through
the tenderloin roll, and marked the ruddy juices that oozed out,
and the puff of odorous steam which ascended as the blade clove
it, "this meat is cooked hunter like, and sort of encourages the
teeth to git into the center of it. I have often noted that cookin'
was a kind of gift, and couldn't be larnt out of books no more
than holdin' a rifle or featherin' a paddle properly can be larnt
in the settlements. The Lord gives one man one set of gifts and
another another, and cookin' and huntin' are things of natur', and
not of readin', and they don't often go all of them to one man,
although in yer case, Henry, the Lord has been very marciful and
gracious-like in his treatment of ye,—for I have heerd ye are a
great scholar, and love the knowledge that the schools give; and
I have many things I want to ax ye of—things I have heerd, but
that seem onreasonable to me; but, depend on it, Henry, the best
gift the Lord has given ye is yer love of natur' and the things that

go with it—a keen eye, a quick finger, a strong back, and a conscience that can meet him in the solitude of these waters and hills
and not be afeared; for a wicked man can't bear the presence of
the Maker of those solitudes, as I have good reason to know"—
and here the old man paused a moment and gazed steadily into the
fire—"yis," he resumed, "it is wonderful that he should have gin
ye the love of books and of natur' both, but I dare to say, he has
his favorites, as I have often noted mothers have among their children, and I can see jest how it may be with him; but how he came
to give ye the gift of cookin' with all the other ones, is wonderful,
and I can't understand it, but"—

A long, loud cry, beginning with a thin whine and swelling up
into a terrific yell, arose into the still air, from the other side of
the lake, held possession of the atmosphere for a full minute, then
died away in successive echoes, leaving the stillness deeper than
before the terrible sound disturbed it and broke suddenly in upon
the old man's speech. For a full minute he sat motionless, with
his fork half way between the plate and his mouth, and his mouth
half opened to receive it, and not till the last mimic imitation of
the frightful scream had died away along the hills that bordered
the head of the lake, did a muscle of his figure move.

"Yis, I know the varmint, and an ugly one he is, too. I heerd
him in the balsam thickets as I come down the inlet, and he trailed
me for a full mile, as they will when hungry; but the cretur' was
too cowardly to show himself in the mash where the moon would
tech him, for a panther has a keen nose for the smell of powder,
and he scented the muzzle of my rifle and knowed I had a wepon.
I hoped he would show himself a minit, or that the swish of the
mash grass as he tramped through it would make a line for me,
for I thought I knowed his whine, and I said to myself, if he gives
me half a chance I'll let light into him, and sort of square accounts
with the cretur that's been some time standin'—but he is a cowardly chap and"—

Again the terrible scream leaped into the air,—this time wild
and savagely fierce at the start, and so harsh that it seemed to tear
the silence into shreds in very fury; and the last hoarse aspiration
of it was so terrible in its wrathful strength that the trees, water
and air seemed to shrink back and shiver in terror at its injection
into the peaceful atmosphere.

"Aye, aye! I know ye now," continued the old man, "and a truer hound than ye murdered for me eleven year ago, come next month, never nosed a track or guarded a hunter's camp. Ye can yell till ye are hoarse, but if the Lord spares this old body, and my eyes don't get dim for another month, I'll look ye up some day and give ye the contents of a grooved barrel that carries a half-ounce bullet, and chambers eighty grains of powder, and ye shall larn the difference between a hunter used to the sights and a poor hound that has nothin' but his teeth and his courage to fight ye with. I guess," continued the old man, as he rose to his feet, "I had better bring up my pack and my rifle, for I noted by the direction the echoes took that the brute yender is trailin' down the lake, and he may cross the outlet at the foot and scout up this side, for his cry shows he is hungry, and he has seen our fire and may think that he can play his capers on us; but he will find the two liveliest morsels he ever tried to put his teeth into, the varmint!" and laughing to himself at his own thought he started for the beach.

"Henry," said he, as he stood leaning over the end of his boat, "come here and we will hist this boat into camp. I dare say I am foolish, but somehow I sorter feel that this lake shore isn't quite the spot to leave an honest man's boat on. I can remember when to have done it would have cost a man his boat and scalp, too, onless the Lord marcifuly kept his eyes open by dreams."

In a moment the boat was placed where the old man wished it, and setting his back against its side for a support, he unlaced his moccasins, and thrust his smoking feet out toward the fire. Taking a pipe from my pocket, I filled it with a choice brand of tobacco I had in my pouch, and proffered it to him.

"Thank ye, thank ye, Henry," said he, as he made a motion of rejection of the offer with his hand, "I thank ye for the kindness ye mean in yer heart, but if it be all the same to ye I won't take it. I know it is a comfort to ye, and I am glad to see ye enjoy it, but I have never used the weed; not for the reason that I had a conscience in the matter, but because the Lord gave me a nose like a hound's, and better too, I dare say, for I doubt if a hound knows the sweetness of things, or can take pleasure from the scent that goes into his nostrils. But he has been more marciful to man—as it was proper he should be—and gin him the power to know good and evil in the air; and smellin' has always been one of my gifts,

and I couldn't make ye understand, I dare say, the pleasure I've
had in the right exercise of it. For ye know that natur' is no more
bright to the eye than it is sweet to the nose; and I've never found
a root or shrub or leaf that hadn't its own scent. Even the dry moss
on the rocks, dead and juiceless as it seems, has a smell to it, and
as for the 'arth I love to put my nose into the fresh sile, as a city
woman loves the nozzle of her smellin' bottle. Many and many a
time when alone here in the woods have I taken my boat and gone
up into the inlet when the wild roses was in blossom, or down into
some bay where the white lily cups was all open, and sot in my
boat and smelt them by the hour, and wondered if heaven smelt
so. Yis, I have been sartinly gifted in my nose, for I've always
noted that I smelt things that the men and women I was guidin'
didn't, and found things in the air that they never suspicioned of,
and I feered that smokin' might take away my gift, and that if I
got the strong smell of tobacco in my nose once I should never
scent any other smell that was lesser and finer than it.—So I have
never used the weed, bein' sort of naterally afeerd of it; but what
is medicine for one man may be pisen for another, as I have noted
in animils, for the bark that fattens the beaver will kill the rat; and
so ye must take no offence at what I've said, but smoke as much
as ye feel moved to, and I will scent the edges of the smell as it
comes over my side of the fire, and so we'll sort of jine works—
as they say in the settlements—ye do the smokin' and I'll do the
smellin', and I think I've got the lightest end of the stick at that."
And the old man laughed in every line of his time-wrinkled face,
at the smartness of his saying.

Chapter VI

THE OLD TRAPPER'S AMBUSH.

"I am out of humanity's reach;
I must finish my journey alone,
Never hear the sweet music of speech—
I start at the sound of my own."

—Cowper.

So we sat on either side of the fire, filled with that contentment which pervades the mind when the body has eaten its fill of hearty food, and the process of digestion is going forward under the conditions of perfect health and agreeable surroundings. For several minutes we sat in silence, too physically happy on my part to think; and the old trapper seemed to have undergone a change of mood, for the play of humor had left his features, and his countenance had settled into a solemn repose.

"I was thinkin'," he said at length—"I was thinkin' of things that happened here long years ago, when I fust come through this lake. I can tell ye, Henry, strange doin's have been done here, and my thoughts have been on the back trail for several days now, and I had a feelin' come to me that I oughter visit this lake, and sorter see how things looked; for there's a grave over there on the pint, that I made with my own hands, and I buried the body of a man in it that had no mourner at his funeral, onless me and my hound, there, might be counted as sech. And I thought I would come through here and see if the grave wanted mendin', although I dare say it lies quiet enough, and ondistarbed, for I built it up in good shape, and sodded it over as the man gave me word to do;— not that he ordered it, but because I knowed it was his wish, for he said the day he died: 'I wish when I am gone my grave might be sodded as they sod them down on the coast where I was born.' And I said to him, 'Don't worry on that score, for I will make it as ye tell me, so far as me and the hound can do it;' and then he told me how he wanted it done, and I will say he talked rational-like from the way he looked at it, and I did it jest as he told me, as the hound there would bear witness if he could speak; and somehow, latterly I got the feelin' into me that I oughter come through here, and sort of see to it, and that's the reason that I am here, although sence meetin' you I have wondered if I warnt brought here to meet the livin' and not the dead; for the Lord don't always tell what he starts us on a journey for, or what we are to find at the other end of it, for the tarmination of things is marcifully hidden from the beginnin', and the two ends of a trail never look alike."

While the Old Trapper had been thus moralizing, he had risen to his feet, and turning round with his back to the fire he stretched a hand out toward the lake, saying:—

"It is not often, Henry, that ye see so bright a moon as that, even here in the woods where the air is as pure as the Lord can make it; and it calls up memories. It is eleven year this very night that me and the hound slept here, and a solemn night it was, too, for the man had died at sunset, and his body lay right there where the moon whitens the 'arth by that dead root.—God of heaven, Henry, what is that!"

The old man's startled ejaculation brought me to my feet as if the panther were on me, and glancing at the spot he had indicated by his looks and gesture, as the exclamation tore out of his mouth, I beheld only the scattered portions of the KEG. Not knowing what to make of the old man's excited action, I said:—

"That? that is only a keg I picked up in the lake this evening."

For a full minute the Old Trapper stood gazing steadfastly at it, and then he stepped to the spot where the remnants of the keg lay, and picking up a stave he contemplated it a minute or two in grave and solemn silence, and then returning to the fire he re-seated himself on the log, and still holding the piece of wood in his hand, said:—

"The ways of the Lord is mysterious, and his orderin's past findin' out; and some of his creturs are born for good and some for evil, and how he ontangles the strands in the end is beyond our knowin'. But perhaps in the long run, he brings the wrong to the right, and so makes the evil in the world to praise him. Ah me! ah me! what a load the man carried while off the trail, like a blind moose walkin' in a circle, but before he tired I reckon he struck the blazed line that led him to the Great Clearin'. Leastwise, it looked so." And the old man paused, gazing fixedly at the bit of the keg that he held in his hand. In a moment he resumed: "I have a mind, Henry, to tell ye the story of the man who owned that keg once, as far as I know it, and onless ye feel sleepy-like I will tell ye what happened here years ago, and what I know of the man whose body lies buried there on yender pint—for a strange tale it is, and a true one, and the teachin's of it is solemn."

I was thoroughly awake, by this time, and urged the old man to proceed. After a moment's silence, he began:—

"Well, it's now eleven years gone, that I was drawin' a trail through the woods from east to west, and I did a good deal of my boatin' in the night, for the moon was full, and I always had a sort of hankerin' for the night work ever sence I slept on the boughs; for natur' looks one way in the day-time, and another way in the night-time, and no one knows how sweet she can be to the nose, and how pleasant to the ears, and how han'some to the eyes, onless he has seen her face, and heerd her voices, and smelt her sweet smells, in the night season. I've always noted that those who knowed natur' only by day-light, knowed only half her ways, and less than half, too, for that matter. For in the evenin' she gits familiar and confidential-like with one, and talks to him of herself and her ways as she never does in the day-time. For natur' has a great many secrets, and she's timid as a young faan, and ye've got to creep into thickets, and lay yer boat up under the banks of streams, and lie down in the mash grass when all is dark and still, if ye want to hear her whisper to ye of her innermost feelin's. The Lord only knows how many times I have ambushed her in her hidin' places as a Huron would a camp, and caught her at her pranks. Ah, Henry, ye have no idee how many things I have larnt of her in the night-time, or how frisky and solemn, both, natur' can be betwixt the settin' and risin' of the sun.

Well, as I was sayin', I'd been over to the east boundaries of the woods, nigh on to the Horricon waters, where I did a good deal of my early scoutin', to sorter see how the brooks and wood-ways looked agin, but it was a sorry time I had on it, for the settlers had pushed in, and their mills was on every stream, and their painted housen stood under the very trees where I used to cook my venison with no sights or sounds around save those that natur' herself made. And ye can well believe, Henry, that I was glad to git away from what I went to see and be back here where my ears couldn't hear the sound of axes and the failin' of trees—yis, I was mighty glad to git back where things was quiet and peaceful-like, and the cruelties and devilments of men that have no respect for things the Lord has made hadn't come to disturb the habits of natur'.

Well, as I was sayin', it was eleven years back, and in this very month, and well on in the night, that I came down the inlet yender into this lake. And the moon was nigh on to her full, and everything looked solemn and white jest as they do to us now, and the Lord knows I leetle thought to meet mortal man in these solitudes when I run agin what I am. to tell ye of.

I was paddlin' down this side of the lake, keepin' well under the shore, list'nin' and thinkin', and happy in my heart as a rat in the water, when I heerd the strangest sounds I ever heerd come out of bird or beast. It was a kind of murmurin' noise that run out into the stillness an' sorter capered round a minit, an' then run back where it started from. Ye better believe, Henry, I sot and listened as a man listens scoutin' alone in the night time in these woods, when he gits a sound in his ears that he can't make out. Yis, I sot and listened ontil I was nothin' but ears, and the very stillness beat on the narves of my head as I have heerd the roll of the waves on the lakes beat on the beach. But for the life of me I couldn't make it sound nateral, nor tell what animil it belonged to, and it took the conceit out o' me to larn that there was a cretur in the woods whose mouth didn't tell me its name and habits.

Arter a while I got the true direction of it, for a sound goes as straight from its startin' to the ear as a bee from a wind-fall or burnt clearin' goes to its hole in the beech, and I said to myself as I lifted my rifle to my knee, that I would ambush the cretur and find out what mouth had a language in it that old John Norton couldn't tell the meanin' of. So I laid my boat up in the direction of the sound as if my life depended on the proper use of the paddle. I hadn't gone more than ten rods afore the noise stopped, but I'd fixed it in the line of a dead Norway and I knowed I could put my boat inside of fifty feet of where the cretur lay. I never acted more sarcumspectly nor fetched an ambushment more easy and sartin', and in a shorter time than it takes me to tell ye I had my boat under the pint of that bank there within ten feet of the shrubs, with my finger on the trigger of a rifle that goes easy in an onsartin ambushment. There I sot a full minit knowin' I was inside of fifty feet of the cretur, with my eyes and ears as open as they should be in such sarcumstances. Then I heerd a a kind of crawlin' sound as if the brute or reptile was trailin' himself along the sand; and I knowed if the wiggle of a bush would give me the line I could open a hole through him. It might have been ten feet that the cretur crawled and than he stopped, but I had fixed him well in mind and felt sartin I could drive the lead where it ought to go. I had got the breech of my rifle half way to my face, and my cheek was settling to the stock, when the cretur opened his mouth, and by the Lord of Marcy, Henry, *I diskivered I had ambushed no animil at all, but a mortal man!"*

Long before the Old Trapper had got to this point of his narrative I had become profoundly interested in his recital. For he told the story as men born to the woods tell their tales of personal adventure—with a natural eloquence of tone, feature and gesture which only those have whose experiences have been narrow but intense, and who speak from the simple earnestness of untutored and therefore unfettered power. His narrative had been told from the beginning in two languages; one verbal and the other pantomimic, and he had carried me along with his story as it advanced as much by that which addressed the eye as by that which entered the ear. He had gathered warmth and energy of expression as he had gone on, until I found myself moving in sympathy with the visible action of his features, body and hands; and when he reached the climax of his discovery, I shared to the full in the excitement of his pantomimic action, and doubt if the shock of surprise which he had experienced eleven years before in his boat under the bank, on the point which lay in the moonlight full in view, was much greater at the startling discovery he had made, than was mine. So we sat looking full at each other across the camp-fire, our faces tense with mutual excitement, as if we were actual sharers in the astonishing discovery.

"Yis, Henry, a *man* was there, a man on that pint where I expected to find only an animil; and his words, as they came out of his mouth into the still air of the night, strong and clear as a man in the rapids calling for help, were words of prayer. I've been, Henry, in many ambushments in the seventy years I've lived, and I've been in peril from inimies behind and afore; and more than once have I met the rage of man and beast and been brought face to face with death onexpectedly; but never since my eyes knowed the sights, so my life depended on the proper use of my faculties, was I ever so taken onawares or onbalanced as I was under the bushes, there on yender pint eleven years gone, when I heerd the voice of that man I had mistook for an animil, break out in prayer. It was of the Lord's own marcy, Henry, that I was not a murderer of my kind, for my finger was on the trigger as I told ye, and my eye was getting onto as trusty a barrel as man ever hefted, when He opened the cretur's mouth with the sound of His own name. For a minute the blood stopped in my heart, and my hair moved in my scalp; and then I shook like a man with the chills, ontil I drew from the guard of my rifle a finger that had never quivered before, for fear I should explode the piece and disturb the man in his worship.

I sot and heerd the man from beginnin' to end, and I larned, under the bushes that night, how hard-put a mortal may be by reason of his sin. For the man prayed for help as one calls to a comrade when his boat has gone down under him in the rapids, and he knows he must have help or die. I've been a prayin' man, Henry, as one should be who lives here in the woods where the Spirit of the Lord is everywhere and in all things; but I never prayed as that man prayed, and it larned me that what is prayin' to one man isn't prayin' to another, for the natur' of our wants settle the natur' of our prayin', and the habits of our life makes the trail to His marcy level or steep. And this man was climbin' a steep trail, and his soul was strugglin' on a hard carry, I tell ye; and the words of his cry came out of his mouth like the words of one who is lost onless somebody saves him. It's dreadful for a man to live in sech a way that he has to pray in that fashion; for we ought to live, Henry, so that it is cheerful-like to meet the Lord, and pleasant to hold converse with him.

So I sot in my boat ontil he was done, and then I hugged myself close in under the bushes, for I heerd him coming down toward the shore, for I knowed be must pass nigh where I lay in the ambushment. And he did,—aye, so nigh that I could have teched him with my paddle, and he had something heavy in his arms, for he staggered as he went by, as if put to it for strength. In a minit I heerd him shove a boat out of the bushes onto the water, and gettin' in, he pushed off onto the lake. He led straight off into the center of it, and I trailed him in his wake, for the moon had got back of the mountain here to the right, and I was determined to see what his queer goin's-on meant. Well, when he had come nigh to the middle of the lake he laid his paddle down, and lifted somethin' into the air, and turned it up endwise and poured what was in it out. I larnt, afterwards, what it was he lifted into the air, and what it was he poured out of it, for he told me with his own lips, and under sech sarcumstances, and at a time, when mortals are apt to tell the truth; for he told me on his death-day, when he lay dyin', and I never knowed a man, white or redskin, that didn't talk straight as an honest trapper countin' his pelts, when he had come to the last blaze on the trail, and his feet stood on the edge of the Great Clearin'.

Chapter VII

FINDING THE MISER.

"Sagacious hound."

—*Virgil.*

Well, I didn't make myself known to him that night, for I felt onsartin' as to the natur' of the man; and beside, I conceited I had no right to step in suddenly upon a man in the midst of his troubles, of whatever sort they might be;—for it always seemed to me that a mortal had a right to have ownership of his own grief, and to shet the door of it agin' the whole world, as much as a hunter in his own camp has a right to shet the door of his lodge. So I shied off farther into the lake and made camp for the night, or what there was left of it, on the island yender.

Well, in the mornin' I bestirred myself, and started my fire ostentatious-like on the side of the island next the p'int, and it made as much smoke as if it had been built by a boy from the settlements, or a college lad in his first trip to the woods, whose tongues run to words, and whose fires are all smoke,—for I wanted to call his eyes over my way and let him know that there was a human on the lake, and one that didn't seek concealment like a thievin' half-breed on an honest trapper's line; for a fire here in the woods is like the little keerds that the gals in the settlements, I have been told, send round to their friends to ax them to drink tea with them, or jine in a jig; a gineral invite to come in and feel at home. So I piled on the timber in a wasteful way, and dropped on a bit of punk now and then, until, 'twixt the blaze and the smoke, I warrant a hunter's eye, even in peace time, not to say a scout's when the redskins are loose, could have seen it ten miles away. But the man on the p'int never took the hint, and well enough he mightn't, for I afterwards larned that he never saw either blaze or smoke, for he was lyin' in his lodge back there in the swale, with his thoughts far away, and his eyes on other lights than such as the hands of man build.

Well, I cooked my breakfast for the hound there and me, and while we were eatin' it we both kept thinkin' of the man on the p'int; for a dog of breedin' knows what his master's thinkin' about, and I could tell by the movements of the hound's nose that the Lord was blowin' knowledge to him from the other side of the lake, and that his thoughts were not on the meat he was eatin', but over there where him and me had fetched our ambushment the night before. So arter we had finished eatin', and cleaned things up, we stood around awhile and kept our eyes on the p'int for some friendly sign, and both me and the hound felt sort of disappinted-like, and the least bit oneasy in mind as to what it all meant; for it seemed mighty queer that the man should make no sign, not to say show himself, when he must have knowed that we wanted to be neighborly. So arter a while I put off toward the p'int, determined to see for ourselves what sort of a cretur' he was, whose behavior had been so mighty onusual the night afore, And I paddled over straight for the bushes where I knowed his boat was, and, sure enough, there it was plain in sight, where I felt it must be.

Then I went ashore and began to poke around, and the trail was plain enough for a man from the settlements to follow with his eyes half shet; for it led from the boat straight up the hill, under the pines and down into the swale back of it. So I pushed along, keeping an eye open for the shanty that I knowed must be nigh, and soon sot my eyes on it, sure enough; but it was no shanty at all, only a mis'rable old tent. I will confess, Henry, that it rather sot me agin the man, whoever he was, when I saw him livin' shet up in an onventilated canvass bag, like a rat in his hole in the spring freshets, when he might have housed himself in a bark lodge, dry and airy, with one side open as a house always should be, arter my way of thinkin'; for it's a great blessin' to be able to see the bigness of the world in which you are livin', and breathe the air as the Lord blows it to ye fresh and strong from the slope of mountains and the cool water level. And I conceit that whoever lives in a canvas shed, that's damp and swashy as last year's mash-grass, must be a very senseless or wicked bein', who don't know how handsome the world is, or else wants to hide himself from the eyes of man, and of the Lord, too, for that matter; for an honest man in the woods builds his lodge so he can see and be seen by day and by night, because he loves the sun and sky by day and the stars by night, and has no reason to hide himself or his traps from the Lord, or from his own kind,—which is open and noble-like, as I understand it. So when I seed the mis'rable and nasty old tent, where the bark was plenty and willin' to be peeled, I felt suspicious of the man, and conceited' that his' morals wasn't what they should be. But in spite of my suspicionin' I detarmined to go on and nose the man out; and I said to myself: 'What right have ye, Old John Norton, to sit in jedgment on a fellow mortal, and before even ye have seed him. It may be the man is ignorant of the ways of the woods, and knows no better nor a babe how to care for himself; or perhaps he has been onfortunit and needs help more than jedgment.'

So I pushed ahead and laid my hand on the rag of a door and drew it aside in a frank sort of a way, and, by the Lord, Henry, the man lay dead before me! Leastwise I thought he was dead, for his eyes was half shet and half open, as a dead man's should be who has died onattended, and his face was as white as the moss on the rock when the moonshine is on it. Well, Henry, it was a solemn sight I can tell ye, and one that made me ashamed of my suspicionin' of the man, and I trust the Lord forgave me the wicked thought I had bad of a fellow mortal because he hadn't showed himself on the p'int, or called on me at my camp, when all the time the hand of death was heavy on him, and his legs were as strengthless as the reeds on the mash when the frost has smitten them.

Well, I stood at the door of the tent and I onkivered my head, as a mortal should in sech solemn sarcumstances, for I verily thought the man was dead; but the hound, there, knowed better, for the Lord has given a sense in sech things to a dog that he withholds from the master, for the hound arter standin' respectful-like behind me a minit, as if he would not be too forrud, or shame me by his better knowledge, pushed in to the side of the body and put his nose to the cheek and then just turned his eyes up to me and wagged his tail. Ah me, it's wonderful what larnin' the Lord has given to the creturs he has made, and how often they know more than their masters; and here was a dog who knowed the livin' and the dead better than I did, though the body was the body of a mortal, and not of his kind.

Well, when I seed the hound move his tail, happy-like, I knowed the man was not dead, however nigh he might be on to it; and so I stepped in quick as powder ever burnt and histed the man up, and took him in my arms, and carried him out of the mis'rable tent into the fresh, cool air, and laid him down in the warm sunshine on the p'int, and fell to chafin' his legs and his wrists, and pressin' on his chest, and sprinklin' water in his face; and I blowed in his nostrils, and did as a man should in such sarcumstances to one of his kind.

But he was mighty weak, and all the strength he had was in his eyes, for he couldn't move hand or foot, more than a buck with a bullet through his spine the mornin' arter he is shot. And it was a very solemn sight to see a full-grown man lyin' on the sand with all natur' lively around him, and he onable to move a leg, or lift a finger; and it showed that the body of a mortal has no more life in it than a last year's beaver's hide, when his sperit has left it; and it was awful-like to see a fellow bein' dead in every member of his mortal frame but his eyes, and all there was of himself lookin' steadily out of them at ye. But I felt he would fetch around arter awhile, for the sun was warm and the wind fresh, and I bolstered him up so it would blow straight into his mouth and nostrils, and I said to myself, if natur' can't bring him to, nothin' can. And so I felt cheerful-like, and pretty sartin that between the sun and warm sand and wind we would get his members warmed up and agoin' agin afore long; and the hound thought so too, for when the man fust opened his eyes the animil knowed it was a good sign as well as I did, for the cretur no sooner saw them open naterally, than he scooted a circle round the body in the sand lively as a young pup at play, and then he stopped in his foolishness and let a roar out of his mouth that might have been heerd over to Salmon Lake 5 and then he came back and sot down on his hanches close by the man, and watched him as arnestly as I did. Every few minits he would look up at me with a happy sort of look in his eyes and fetch a wag or two, with his tail; and it was mighty cheerful and encouragin to see the animil act so, and made me feel sort of chirpy myself, as I sot in the sand watchin' the man, for I knowed the hound was a truthful dog, and was wise in his gifts, and wouldn't lie agin the vardict of them, and I conceited that the man would pick up and be able to talk, if the dog said so.

"I ONKIVERED MY HEAD." PAGE 70.

"Well, arter a while the man begun to pick up for sartin, for the blood come back into his skin, and his fingers begun to open and shet easy-like, and he put his tongue out and wet his lips naterally as a man does arter sleep in a hot lodge. I sarched my pack and found some tea a city woman gave me the summer afore for a sarvice I done her on the Racquette, which was no more than any man would do for a woman, but which she said she should never forgit till her dyin' day,—and I guess she never will, for I found somethin' she had lost that lay near her heart, and I never knowed a white woman, or squaw, neither, for that matter, forgit a man who done them a sarvice in that direction;—well, as I was sayin', I sarched for the tea the city woman had given me, and steeped a cup of it for the man on the sand, and I made it strong as the leaf would make it, for I knowed it would help natur' to rally, and make him strong enough to take nourishment, and set his tongue goin', if such a thing could be by the Lord's appintment.

So I gave him the drink, and it took hold on him at once. It was really amazin' Henry, how the yarb put life into him as if it had the Lord's own power to call the soul back into the mortal frame and set the members of it workin'. Yis, it was a marvel to see the power that natur' had put into a few withered leaves—for the more he drank the better he felt, and by the time he had come to the bottom of the cup I could see that the man was nigh himself agin, and likely enough to begin to talk; and sure enough, in a minit he made a effort to speak, and arter one or two trials he got his tongue used to the motions, and said:—

"Old man, who be ye, that has called me back from the gates of death and summoned me from the borders of the grave?"

"My name," I said, "is John Norton, and I be nobody but a hunter and trapper who has done nothin' but live in a nateral way and sarve his kind when the Lord gave him a chance; and as for bringin' ye back from the border of the grave, I think ye was pritty nigh onto it, and me and the hound yender, and the tea I steeped for ye, did mayhaps give ye a lift in the right direction—though it musn't be overlooked, if ye are cur'us in the matter; that the sun and wind done their part to bring ye to; and I dare say the Lord in his marcy has done more than us all, for ye sartinly would have died if he hadn't given the hound the sense to know the dead from the livin' and helped us in our endivers. And now, friend, what may yer name be, and what game did ye have in mind when ye pushed yer trail from the settlements into this lonely lake; for I see from the signs, that ye know nothin' of the woods, and I marvel why a man of yer ignorance should leave the hants of yer kind, and I dare say kindred, and risk yerself in these out-of-the-way places, which be pleasant to those who know them, but risky to them that doesn't; so I ax ye yer name, and why I find ye here alone and unprotected as if ye hadn't a friend on the arth."

"John Norton," said the man, "my name is Roberts, John Roberts; and I have not a friend on the earth, nor do I deserve one, for I have forfeited the love of all that ever loved me, by my evil acts, and the Lord has visited upon me the punishment I deserved by separating me from them. Yea, out of my sins has come judgment, and my evil thought has been the pit into which I have stumbled. But the marcy I had forfeited has been shown me, in my guilt, and the peace of the Spirit that made and lives in the universe has been breathed into me from these mountains and the sky and the majesties of nature in the presence of which, glad that my mortal life is ended, I lie dying;" and the man turned his eyes on the objects he named, with the look of a hound in them when he meets the pleased face of his master.

"John Roberts," I said, "I do not understand ye, for the beauty of natur' is sech as to make men wish to live and not to die, and though I trust I may be willin' to go when He calls, still I can't conceit of any place pleasanter or more cheerful-like for a human bein' to live in than these woods, and I hope He will let me stay here, scoutin' round, as long as His plans techin' me allow of; and, as for that matter, if He should forgit us altogether I don't conceit that me and the hound would be very onhappy or feel cheated-like, but would hold it as a kind of a marcy, and keep on enjoyin' ourselves and sarvin' Him in the way of natur's app'int-ment; and as for friends, I haven't an inimy in the world but a thievin' Huron I caught on the line of my traps, last winter, and shortened his left ear half an inch with a bullet, and a mis'rable half-breed or two I've larnt the commandments in a similar man-ner. But outside of these, me and the hound there are in peace with all the 'arth, and feel cheerful and pleasant-like toward every livin' bein', except the panthers,—yis, always exceptin' the pan-thers, that we keep a kind of runnin' account with, as the pedlars say in the settlements, and square up whenever we git a chance."

"Ye see, Henry," continued the old man "I wanted to chirk him up as much as I could, because he was mighty weak still, and I thought that low sperits would sot him back agin, so even the hound and me couldn't bring him to; and so I talked the least bit frisky-like, and took on as if I felt ondistarbed. But he knowed better all the time; for he looked at me with his eyes fixed solemnly on my face and said:—

'Old man, I know you can't understand, because you have lived an innocent life, and according to the light you had you have walked in the path of righteousness, and the peace of the upright is in your heart, and the light of it is over all the world, and makes it desirable to your eyes. And I can well understand that you need no other life than the one you lead, or other heaven than the lovely scenes which your gifts and your manner of life have taught you so well to enjoy; and I can understand, too, how you cannot grasp the meaning of a guilt as those who sin against light feel it: the guilt of a man who has resisted God and hardened his nature by a cursed passion, and hated what he should have loved, and loved with lusting what he should have hated—for you have been as a child, and the Kingdom of Heaven has come to you with the years, because your aging took not the simple innocency of childhood from you. But I have lived so that memory is only fuel to remorse, and the earth a constant reminder of my guilt; and hence I would seek my heaven in the forgetfulness of death, and anticipate another land beyond the grave, in hopes of finding escape from what torments me here, and having ministered unto my life the boon of a new start. And you must know that there are those in the world beyond the grave whom I have wronged, and the load of their wronging lies heavy on my soul. I would find them, and on my knees ask their pardon; for, old man, even God himself cannot undo the structure of our minds, nor perform duty for us, and I feel that the forgiveness of Heaven cannot make me happy until I have the forgiveness of my wife whom I deserted, and of my child whom I, with curses, refused to see in her dying hour.

And you should know, old man, that I am dying, and I long to die; nor do I ask aught save that I may have strength to tell you my story, and give you a few directions; for it will ease my soul to talk while dying, and I know it will delight you to hear of the goodness of that God whom you, in simple reverence, worship, and to learn from the lips of a dying sinner that the woods you so love have been to him the means of his salvation. So sit you down, old man, and listen closely, for I am weak, and I will tell you the story of my life;—why I am here, and what you are to do with what is left of me and mine when I am gone from here, as I soon shall be, forever.'

"Well, Henry, I saw that the man was in solemn arnest, and I knowed the Lord was apt to give a mortal nigh death a foreknowin' of the time and order of things techin' his departur', and I conceited the man was right in his idees, and that it would be onreasonable to resist him; so I sot down on the sand by his side and said, 'Well, friend, I allow there's reason in your words, and John Norton is not the one to arger agin a dyin' man nor disturb his thoughts with foolish talkin'. And it may be ye have come nigh the end of the trail, as ye say, and if so I sartinly advise ye to onload yerself of whatever bears heavy on ye; for a man should enter the Great Clearin' with nothin' heavier than his rifle about him, and ready for whatever sarvice the Lord app'ints. And as to the directions, ye may give me as many as ye have to tell, and if it be within range of mortal power it shall all be done as ye tell me; for I have sot beside many a dyin' man arter the scrimmage was over, and heerd his words, and not one, white or redskin, friend or inimy, can rise in the jedgment and say John Norton didn't do jest as he was told to do. So ye jest go ahead and ease yer mind, John Roberts, and me and the hound will listen, and as we larn yer wishes so will we do, even if the traps aint sot on the line next winter, or the trail of your errand takes us into the onnateral noise and diviltry of the settlements.'

So I promised the man, Henry, and kept my word, as the hound, there, knows, for he heerd it all and seed it all arterwards, and it was done jest as the man appinted. And this is what he told me as he lay on the sand, with me and the hound listenin'.

Chapter VIII

THE MISER'S CONFESSION.

"One impulse from a vernal wood
May teach you more of man,
Of moral evil and of good,
Than all the sages can."

—Wordsworth.

"My father, John Norton, was a miser, although the world never knew it; but he loved money, and all his life was spent in getting it. He lived to be an old man, and when he died he was buried from the meeting-house—for he was a deacon in the church—and the minister preached the sermon, and told the people of his thrift and economy, of his industry and sobriety, and held him up as an example, when I knew, and all his friends knew, that he was sober when others drank, simply because he was too stingy to drink, and that his industry was all selfish, and that his economy was miserly. I only tell you this to let you know whence I got my love of money, and how the lust of gain came in me. It was born in me, John Norton, as much as the power of scenting was born in your hound yea, given me at birth from the miserly nature and habits of a father who was a church member, and whose character and mode of life were praised by the minister when they buried his body.

He left me all his property, for I was his only child; and no one save me ever knew how much it was, for it was largely in gold coin that he had hidden away, and which he told me of, and where to find it, by whispering it in my ear when he was dying. I was thirty years of age before he died, and the property fell to me; and until I had the gold myself, and had seen it and counted it, I had lived a happy life; for I was married to an angel, and had three children, and a happier family never lived than we were before the gold came to me. But no sooner had I gotten it into my possession than I began to love it. Yea, the sight of the coin started the lust for it in me, and woke to full life the awful appetite for it which was in him and which he had transmitted to me. And the love for that gold grew on me as I handled it;—and handle it I did, until it became a passion with me. I used to get up nights when my wife was sleeping and go down cellar where I kept it in a large pot, and count it over, and push my hands into it, and laugh to hear it rattle, and to see it shine in the candle light. And the love of it grew and grew and grew, until I loved nothing else. And with the growth of the dreadful lust in me there grew a suspicion of men and women, because I had got it into my head that they would steal it, until at last I grew suspicious of my own wife and children, even to such a degree that I drove them out of the house and forbade them ever to cross its threshold again. You say I was mad. Yes, I was mad—mad with the awful madness of one in whose heart is a terrible and wicked love; a love that entices him and seduces him from good unto evil, and finally becomes stronger than conscience—stronger than affection for wife and children— yea, stronger than his fear of God. Yes, I was mad in that way, and the madness grew in its fury until it became a continuous frenzy, and my life one hell of raging fear, suspicion and hatred of my kind. I need not tell you all, for you would not understand it; you could not understand it, for you have never handled money nor known the love of it, and are as a child in your knowledge of such an experience. At last I came to these woods; came driven by the frenzy of fear lest men should steal my money; came, not from the love of nature, or the longing for a peaceful, quiet, innocent life; but in order to be where my money would be safe, for my money was my God, my life, my heaven, and I feared someone would steal it, and so I brought it here because no man was here. How did I bring it? I brought it in a keg; a keg stout and large, and lined with my own hands; and that keg was my altar, my shrine, my God. John Norton, remember it's a dying man that is talking to you, when I tell you that here, on this very beach where I now lie, and you sit, I have sat in the bright sunlight and in the solemn moonlight, too, and counted my money by the hour, and laughed and danced around it as a devil might; yea, I, a mortal man, have danced around a pile of money like a heathen round his idol, with the great blue sky overhead, and beyond the sky, the greater God looking solemnly down with his all-seeing eyes upon me and my gold."

And here the man paused, Henry, a minit, and he panted like a young faan in her fust race with the hounds, for he was overtaskin' his strength, and I feered he would die for sartin if he didn't fetch up a bit and git rested; so I thought I had better give him a lift in the right direction by talkin' a leetle myself, and I drawed at a ventur', like a man who sends the lead by his notions of the sound, when it's too dusky to get his eye into the sights, and said:—

"If I was in your place, Mr. Roberts, I would set down and rest a bit, for ye are travelin' with a big load over a rough carry, if I am any jedge, and ye are gittin' sort of shaky-like in yer legs, and ye will come down in a heap pritty soon if ye don't steady up a bit and take it a leetle easier; for me and the hound mean to fetch ye round yit that is, if the tea don't gin out, and the Lord's app'intments be not agin it. So ye jest hold up a minit or two, and rest while we stir in a few more leaves of the yarb, and steep it for ye easy-like, for tea can't be hurried no more than a slow hound in the beginnin' of a race, before he's got the scent warm in his nose, and his faculties workin'. No, the yarb is spunky and knows its own importance, and won't stand rough treatment; and if ye bile it a bit, its vartu' is gone, for a wallopin' pot spiles the tea; so ye give me and the hound time to do the thing up accordin' to the rules and practices of correct obsarvation, and we will give ye a lift that'll make ye grateful to us both.

I don't catch the pith of yer last sayin' about the eyes of the Lord bein' terrible as he was lookin' at ye; and I can't conceit of it, nohow. Now, the eyes of a panther are terrible, sure enough, and I have lined the sights by them when they barnt a hole in the darkness; and I have had many a clinch with a Huron in a scrimmage, when I was younger, when the blood of his savagery was up, and his eyes was as red as an adder's; but the eyes of the Lord, as I have seed them in the works of his hand, have always been strong, for sartin, but gentle and mild as a mother doe when her faan is friskin' around her, and I can't conceit of the face of the Lord as bein' terrible, nor understand how a mortal could be afeerd to have them on him."

And all the while, Henry, I kept kindlin' the fire for the tea. But the man broke in on me, and said:—

"Old man, leave off preparing that tea and hear me; for naught that you can do will prevent my dying, for it is written that I die this day, and I feel within my soul that my hour is drawing nigh. Leave off your preparations, therefore, for your efforts cannot save me from death, nor would I have it otherwise if I could. I want you to listen and hear my words, nor move again until I am done."

So I sot down agin, and the hound came and sot down on the other side of the man, and then he began to talk:—

"John Norton, I came to these woods a miserable miser. There was in all my life but one love, and that was for money. Money I loved, loved it with all the strength of my nature. For years I had thought of nothing else, and cared for nothing else. For years I had no joy but the fierce joy of seeing it and counting it. To me my money was all there was in the whole universe worth loving,—the one idol of my soul. Well, I brought it here because no man was here, and hence knew it could not be stolen. With it safe, I was happy. With it secure, I asked no higher boon. I was not only a miser, but I was hardened in all my nature. The lust of gold had eaten out all other cravings. All noble affections, all tender sympathies, all truthful qualities, all charities and fine emotions had been by this all-absorbing passion, banished from my bosom. I was only a shell of a man inhabited by one great devil. This devil in me had his fierce joy, his tormenting suspicions, his rending rage, his agonies and his pangs; but no trace of humanity, no fiber of charity, no possibility of peace. Thus possessed, I came to this lake. You must not think I had not been entreated; for man and women had alike been faithful to me, and with prayers, with tears, with warnings and exhortations had they striven to deliver me from the devil within, and bring me to my right mind. But neither man nor woman, neither wife nor child, nor the Spirit of God acting in and through these could make me see the sinfulness of my sin, nor the emptiness of my passion, nor the vanity of my life. These I could resist and had resisted. Man could not master the devil in me nor drive him out of my soul."

"But here the demon was met by other agents and agencies he could not resist, and here the devil in me was mastered. By whom and what? By Nature, I reply, and by the irresistible majesties of God in Nature. Here the greatness of my surroundings made me small, and the immeasurable splendors above me at night, and the glories around me by day, made my gold seem contemptible. Not that these influences came to be felt at once; not that the conviction produced by them was sudden, for it was not; but slowly, subtly, and in a way I could not fight; with a power I could not resist, out of the silence of space, out of the blue sky and the uplifted mountains, out of sunrise and sunset, out of the water and the air, out of the solemn nights and the succession of splendid days there came regeneration to my soul. Within me was born in this mystical way a sense of larger and holier things, and moods of worship, and generous thoughts, and longings for what was fine and far ahead; so that, involuntarily, and before I was aware, a change came to me in my likes and feelings, and I beheld as with eyes newly opened the significance of things, the use of life and the true application of its lessons. I said that my eyes were opened; and they were, so that I who had never thought of the beyond and the coming, but had lived in the here and the now, was compelled by a force within me to look constantly up and ahead into the great unseen and unknown. And this force within me I could not resist. It was stronger than my will and mightier than habit, and, forced by its energy, I yielded. And then out of the unknown and the unseen there came forth, as the blaze of a beacon from darkness and distance, a vision, and it scared me at first to face it, but at last I was able; and the vision that blazed out upon me from the darkness and the distance, terrible in its brightness, was the *Idea of Immortality.*"

"John Norton, this idea haunted me. The idea of life beyond, stretching on forever and forever, unintermittent and endless, lay like a mountain on my guilty soul. And out of the conception came interrogations that searched me through and through like a knife. And out of this searching, amid agony and pangs, was born a Conscience: a Conscience which pinched me like a vice, and wrung groans and cries of remorse out of my mouth, until, at times, the silence of the night was filled with my moaning. It was the silence that did it, old man for the silence was more than silence: it was GOD. I could not fly from it; I could not escape its rebukes; I could not hide myself from its solemn upbraidings. It condemned me for the life I had lived; it upbraided me for the passion I had nursed; it threatened me with the censure of a just and holy verdict. Here, on this point, in the midst of the all-surrounding silence, I found my Judgment Day. Here my mind lost the petty measurement of time, and took to itself in perfect sensing the realization of eternity. Here I wrestled with the Spirit that has not form, and strove with the energy that can never be incarnate: the Spirit of Justice and Love commingled with the energy of God. Here, old man, I strove; here I was overcome; and here I yielded; aye, yielded to a test. And the test was this: that I should deliberately, with my own hands, empty into the waters of this lake the gold I had loved like a devil; and to keep which, without fear of losing it, I had been self-banished from my kindred and kind and had come to this lonely lake. Yes, I yielded; yielded to the power I could not resist; the power of the Lord who made and inhabits these woods, and whose presence I saw and felt in their beauty, and majesty, and silence. And I cried unto Him to whom I had yielded, for strength to do the test; cried unto Him on my knees, with my hands on the keg that held the gold, for strength to deliver my soul from its horrible spell, and pour it—yea, every dollar of it,—into the waters of the lake. And he gave me strength, old man,—even in answer to my prayer did he strengthen me to do the deed, which, being done, delivered me from the spell of the power that had held me, and from the bondage to the terrible lust. And last night the battle was fought, and the victory won, and I was delivered from Hell. For I prayed unto Him, and he listened and heard; and I lifted the keg and carried it to my boat, and paddled to the middle of the lake. And there, with hell and heaven to see, I lifted the keg in my arms and held it out over the water, and poured the gold I had worshipped into its depths. And there and then, when the deed was done, the blessing of the Lord came on me, and His marvelous peace stole into my soul. It came to me from the air, and the water, and the sky; from the bosom of the white moon-lighted stillness; from the motionless woods and the shores; came to me from the nigh and the far; from the air around me and the infinite spaces above and beyond; came to me, Old Trapper, from the outbreathings of that God who is Spirit, and in whom the innocent and the forgiven live, and move, and have being."

Here the man came to a halt, Henry, and he looked into my eyes as if he wanted to see if I understood, and arter a minit or two he said,—

"Old Man, do you understand me?"

"Well," said I to him, "I can't say that the trail of your talk is altogether plain to me, Mr. Roberts, but me and the hound has kept our eyes on ye as ye blazed along on the line, and I guess we have got the gineral direction of it. I can see for sartin that ye had a rough trip, and a heavy pack to carry, and ye must have found it hard backin' at times. It seems to me if ye had onloaded earlier ye would have fetched through in better shape and saved valable time, for ye look to me like a man who hasn't got over the carry 'til dusk, and can't be of much sarvice to the camp 'til another sunrise; but I think ye have got across for sartin and are out of the woods, and that's a good deal to say of a man who has been lost and fooled away half his day by walking in circles, and I rejice that ye are where ye are, and know which way the trail leads arter this and if ye are sartin of the lay of the land ahead and know where the line ye are on leads to, ye oughter feel contented and happy like, as I dare say ye do, Mr. Roberts."

"Yes I do feel contented and happy," said he, "happier than words may tell. My sin has been great, but the mercy of God is greater, and I feel I can trust Him here and beyond. I have lived as no man should live, but here, on this beach today, my life will end, and when I am gone you may think of me, as a sinner whose sin was forgiven and whose soul had found peace."

Arter this he didn't say much for some time but lay with his eyes lookin' up to the sky and a quiet sort of a look on his face. I conceited the man was thinkin' of things, and it may be of people, a good ways off, and that it wouldn't be right to disturb him in his meditations. But arter a while I said to him, for I felt a little oneasy on the subject, for I feered he would forgit it,—"Mr. Roberts, ye spoke about some directions ye wanted to give me, and perhaps ye had better say what ye have in mind on the matter, so me and the hound may know jest what ye want done by and by; for we shall mind and do jest as ye tell us, if it be within the range of our gifts, and death don't overtake us on the arrand."

Well, arter a little while he turned his eyes on me and said:—

I suppose it don't make much difference where or how my body is buried, after I am gone; do, you, Old Trapper?"

"Well, no, I don't think it does, Mr. Roberts, when ye git right down to the gist of the matter; but every cretur' is born with his prejudices, and has his own ideas of what is right and proper teaching things to be done; and I conceit the Lord allows a man to fetch his line about where he pleases in pints of parsonal jedgment: and if I was in yer place I should have my own way about my burial, and have everythin' did straight and systematic-like, accordin' to my own ideas of the thing. Now, me and the hound there, has our own notions about the treatment the mortal frame should receive arter the speerit has left it, and we conceit that it should be treated as a Huron treats his lodge when he is about to move out of it forever. But we can guess our notions wouldn't suit ye nor seem reasonable-like, because ye was edicated another way, and I have always noted that a man sticks to his arly edication as a moose sticks to his gait. So we won't distarb ye with our idees; but do jest as ye tell us to, even if it be agin reason, as me and the hound understand it?"

Well, the man seemed to be sort of encouraged to say his mind out arter what I had said, and arter looking at the sky awhile, with his eyes half shet, he said:—

"Do you know, John Norton, for days I have been haunted with the fear of dying alone. I dare say it is foolish of me, but I can't help it, nevertheless, and I praise the Lord that He has sent you to me in the hour of my need. The sight of your face helps me beyond what I can tell, and the sound of your voice has banished the terrible loneliness from my soul. Yes, I shall die happy, now that the companionship of my kind is given me in death. When I am gone I want you to give me a decent burial, as they do down on the coast where I was born. And the way of it is this: They dress the body in good clothes, and put it in a coffin, and they read a chapter or two from the Bible at the house where the man lived, and the minister prays and the choir sings. Then they take the coffin to the grave and bury it, and they generally have a prayer at the grave; and they sod the grave, and put a slab of stone at the head, and plant flowers on the mound. I know, old man, that you can't do all this, and you needn't try. Only do the best you can, that is all; especially bury me so the wolves can't get my bones, and say a few pious words above the grave."

Well, arter this he said nothin' for a full hour, and I said nothin' neither, for it was plain that his feet was on the very edge of the Great Clearin', and I felt it was nateral for a man standin't at the very end of the trail to want to look around him in silence awhile; and so I said nothin', for I feared to distarb his mind as he stood lookin' into the etarnal world. By and by he said:—

"Old man, the hour is almost come when I must go, and the way ahead is dark. I see no light and no helper. What can I do?"

"John Roberts," I said; for I could see by the look of his face and the fear in his voice, that he was in trouble, like a boy lost in the woods, "stick to the trail and keep your eye on the blazed line of His marcy. Don't hurry, but take it slow and sarcumspectly and trust to the markin's. I have heerd said that the carry ye are on led through a valley, dim and dusky as a stretch of pine land by night, but that the man who stuck to the line would fetch through all right. And remember, that me and the hound isn't far behind, and sartinly the Lord aint far ahead; so stick to the line, and don't swing a foot from the trail, and ye will strike risin' land afore long and see light." And I moved close up to his side and lifted his head into my lap, so he could catch his breath easier; for he was laborin' heavily, and I know'd he couldn't stand it much longer.

So I sot in the sand holdin' his head, and the hound sot at his feet, and we both kept our eyes on the face; and arter our fashion I prayed for the man, and put the case before the Lord in a strong sort of a way, I can tell ye.

Well, arter a while a great change came over his featurs. He opened his eyes and looked into my face in a happy way as if he had seen a new sight, and a smile crept over his lips, and his countenance softened like the clouds arter storm, and he said:—

"Old man, old man, I see light ahead!" And then he drawed a long contented sort of a breath, moved his legs out easily in the sand, rolled his head gently over in my lap as if goin' to sleep, closed his eyes; and his sperit, without groan or struggle, stole out of the body in which it had lodged so long in trouble, and passed through the clear light and the air up to its Maker. And that is the way, Henry, he came to the eend of the trail, and I reckon he found the Lord of marcy waitin' for him at the edge of the Clearin'.

So I sot in the sand, with the head in my lap, closin' his eyes, and the hound, accordin' to his gifts, came and put his nose agin the cheek, and then walked down to the end of the pint, and sot down on his hanches, and lifted his nose into the air and lamented."

Chapter IX

THE DEATH WATCH.

"In vain the she-wolf stands at bay;
The blinded catamount that lies
High in the boughs to watch his prey,
Even in the act of springing, *dies*."

—*Bryant.*

Well, Henry, I didn't do nothin' about the burial until next day, for I thought it looked more decent-like not to hurry the matter of the entarment, and, moreover, I conceited it was no more than reasonable that me and the hound should hold a council over the matter; for there's nothin' helps a man's jedgment more on any pint, whether it be a funeral or a scrimmage, than to set down and talk it over with a companion, and me and the hound has consorted so much together that we understand each other and never differ on the main pints of a case—although I do think that he lost a panther last fall by gittin' the scent wrong eend to in his nose, and leading off like an unlarned pup on the heel of the track; but the hound thought otherwise, and mayhaps I was mistaken. So I went down, on the eend of the pint where he was lamentin' accordin' to his gifts, and put it to him that we had better camp just where we was, on the trail, and lay over till another day, and I give him the reasons for it systematic-like from beginnin' to eend, and made the pints plain accordin' to the natur' of the case, and we both agreed to it. And we jined judgment, furthermore, in this, that the body oughter be carried to a camp and watched and not left on the pint, for fear the varmints would git to it overnight and spile the corpse. So we went back to the body, and carried it to my boat and laid it down on some boughs I had cut for it, and the hound followed on careful-like and sot down at the feet of the body, and I got in at the other eend and shoved off, and so we fetched the dead over the water till we come to this pine knoll, and here me and the hound come ashore with the body, and sot about preparin' for the death-watch we know'd we must hold over night.

Well, Henry, it was sorter new work, ye see, for me and the hound; for though I have buried many a man in the trenches arter the fight, and though I have kivered up a good many redskins off and on in my life, yit I wasn't very handy at the mournin' equipments of the settlements. But I have seed many a gineral laid out on his bier, in the old wars, with his uniform on and his sword by his side, and the death sentries on duty, and the muffled drums all beatin'; and I conceited that though Mr. Roberts wasn't a gineral, nor even a privit in the ranks for that matter, that he should be treated in an honorable way now he was dead.

So I cut some crotches and drove 'em into the ground, and made a frame of small white birches, about the size of a bier, and on these I put a layer of balsam and cedar boughs, and over these I scattered pine tufts ontil I had a bed fit for the dead or livin', gineral or privit, and I laid in plenty of hard wood for my fire, and some pitch knots, for I said to myself, 'if the animils come round I will have to shine up on 'em, and defend the corpse'; for I feared the panthers—for this lake is a great spot for the varmints, and 'leven years ago there was sartinly as many as there is now. And arter I had got the bier ready I laid the body on it, and bolstered the head up nateral-like, and then me and the hound sot down to supper with a dead man at the table. We didn't waste time in the eatin', for the sun was already down, and by the time we had cleaned things up night had come.

Well, Henry, I took my stand at the foot of the bier, and kept my death-watch, rifle in hand, steady as a sentry on duty, save when I stirred the fire or lighted a pine knot. For the animils was oneasy, as they always is when a corpse is round, and I needed the pine knots more than once, and some of the varmints got the tech of lead and the smell of powder that night, I tell ye, for they was full of their devilments, and made me and the hound as wakeful as if we was surrounded by inimies."

"Did you really have to kill any thing?" I asked, speaking for the first time in an hour; for the Old Trapper had told his story with such naturalness of intonation and gesture that he had held me spell-bound by his narrative—for no one could hear him tell the strange tale he was telling and not be carried along by the movement of it,—and now that he was evidently reaching the climax, I feared I should miss some detail of his experience which being omitted would mar the narration, so, hoping to hold his utterance to the line of actual occurrence, I said, "Did you have to kill any thing, that night?"

"Well, yis, I did," he replied. "I bored a hole through a dog-wolf over there on the beach, arter I had borne his onnateral howlin' as long as a mortal could; and I dropped a cat from that dead cedar there, arter me and the hound had stood the stare of her eyes for ten minutes or more, and about two in the mornin', a litter of panthers crawled in on us ontil the bush seemed alive with 'em, and I lifted the scalp of the biggest of the drove, arter he had got within forty feet of the corpse and paid no more attention to the brands I pitched at him than if they was tufts of sod; so with a pine knot all afire, in one hand, to show me the sights, I drove the lead in between his infarnal eyes in a style that taught 'em all manners for the rest of the watch. Yis, Henry, we had a solemn and lively time of it, for sartin, that night, and at times it looked as if there would be no funeral the next day; leastways, none that me and the hound would attend, onless we made one for ourselves; but we stood to our post, and between the brands and the lead and the help of the Lord we brought the body through safe 'til sunrise.

But it was mighty solemn watchin' by the body all by myself on the shores of this lake, here that night; for at times the animils would make the air roar and scream, and the mountains to yelp as if the upper world was inhabited with cats and wolves and panthers, and then they would suddenly become quiet, and the world round about was nothin' but silence with the moon shinin' through it: and the dead man's face was white as the moon and still as the air, for his troubles was over and the marks of them passed from his features when his breath went away. And so me and the hound kept our watch by the dead, 'til the sun riz in the east, and the hour had come for the funeral."

Chapter X

THE FUNERAL.

"And let there be prepared a chariot-bier
To take me to the river, and a barge
Be ready on the river."

—Tennyson.

The first thing to do was to fix on the spot for the grave, which took leetle time to settle, for it seemed natur'l that the body should lie nigh where it had lived; and natur' sartinly had made a fit spot for it jest up on the bluff, off the p'int; for it was clean and sweet there, and the pines was always singin' overhead. And if a man is to be buried underground, arter he is dead, which me and the hound hold to be unreasonable and heathenish-like, I conceit he should be laid in a sightly spot, with a good outlook to it, and not stuck away in a swale or mash as if he was no better nor a cat, or a root hedge-hog. So I shaped me a spade from a slab I rived from a pine the lightnin' had leveled, and digged the grave deep in the dry sand under the pines, and filled it half full of pine stems, and cedartwigs, and other sweet smellin' things that grow around; and on the green stuff I flung in an armful of white lilies I plucked in the bay, to make the bed look cheerful and fittin' for a mortal to lie in. When this was done I come back to this spot and did to my boat what I had done to the grave: made it green, and sweet, and handsome, with the growths of natur' that had pleasant scents in them, until the boat was nigh on to bein' full. And then I lifted the body and laid it at length, and put the hands alongside each other on his breast, and, with the hound in the bow of the boat and me in the starn, I swung out into the lake, and with easy stroke, lined a course straight as an arrow could go toward the p'int. And so, without the presence of wife or child, or kin of any kind to attend him; without bell, or drum, or priest, the man who had desarted his home and fellow-bein's went toward his grave.

Well, arter a while the boat fetched the sand, and the hound got out; and I shoved it up a leetle further and I got out, and liftin' the body in my arms I carried it up the p'int, and climbed the knoll till I come to the grave, and I laid the corpse down on the pine tufts and the lilies. And I recalled all the man had told me about the singin' and the prayer and the Book, and I did the best I could under the sarcumstances, to follow the trail of his directions, and I knowed if I did the best I could accordin' to my gifts, the sperit of the man would overlook the rest; but I felt sartin that somethin' oughter be said out of the ordinary run of human talkin', or the man wouldn't be more than half buried arter 'twas all ended. And the hound seemed to jine with me in the idee, for he looked up in my face in a questionin' way, as if askin' when the sarvice was to begin. So arter a minit I got down on my knees and told the Lord what I thought was jedicious. I think I can recall jest about what I said word for word, for my mem'ry is good, and a man don't talk overfast, Henry, in sech sarcumstances, and it has all come back to me sence I sot here to-night as if it was but yesterday sence I buried the man, and I can give ye the words pretty nigh. Yis, I got down on my knees by the edge of the grave and said:—

"Great Sperit, here lies the body of one of thy creturs. His arthly ways was known to thee, and the wrong of his wickedness was not hidden. He seems to have straightened the trail of his misdoin's in the end, and fetched through to the Great Clearin' as a mortal should. But me and the hound know'd leetle about him, and jest how he came to thy presence we couldn't see, but it sartinly looked hopeful. Here me and the hound has brought his corpse for entarment accordin' to orders, and the trail at this p'int is onsartin', but we mean to fetch through to the eend of this job with thy help. So jest give us a lift at this talkin', that the corpse may have a sarvice as is becomin'. Bless us in our endivers, and let thy peace, which is one, as I understand it, with Natur's, come on this grave I am buildin', and here rest until the Jedgment Day. Then squar' accounts with the man, not by the line of give and take, so much for so much, but by the line of marcy and of overlookin' of scant skins in the man's count; and don't forgit to reckon easily with me and the hound, for we are rather onsartin' consarnin' the blazes on this line, and suspicion we may git wrong eend to before we fetch through. So be marciful to us three;—to the man because of what he did, and to me and the hound for what we didn't know how to do. Keep all varmints from this grave,—seeh as cats and wolves,—especially panthers: onless I am here to attend to them, in which case ye may let them come rampin' round as much as the creturs' please, and I'll agree to keep them orderly. Amen."

"Well, Henry," said the Old Trapper, after a pause, "do you think I did the square thing by the man? I did the best I could accordin' to my gifts and I sartinly trust the corpse was satisfied."

I could see that the Old Trapper was troubled in regard to the matter more than he chose to confess, and knowing how impossible it is for one totally unaccustomed to forms of any kind to fall into the grooves of formal utterance, I could fully understand how profound must have been his embarrassment in attempting to conduct a funeral service according to the rules and methods which prevail in civilized, not to say fashionable communities, and as I looked into the simple, guileless face of the Old Trapper, which showed doubt, perplexity, and pain in its every wrinkle and furrow, I felt that I was authorized to go as far as I could truthfully in the way of comfort, so I said:—

"I think you did excellently, John Norton; and I doubt not the spirit of the man was well satisfied with what you did to honor his body at its burial, and I know that the Lord understood your circumstances and gave you full credit for the beautiful spirit of obedience to the dead man's wishes you showed in following his instruction."

"Well, I am mighty glad ye think so, Henry. I have felt oneasy on the matter for eleven years, for I feerd I had got off the track altogether in the sarvice, for I had a dim line to trail by, as the man's talk wasn't very plain to me to start with, and the hound was no more help in the matter than an unlarnt pup is to a hunter on a dry track. Yis, I sartinly feel easier in the matter arter what ye have said, and the Lord knows I meant only good to the man, and tried to be respectful to the corpse.

"Well, there isn't much more to tell ye. Arter the sarvice I put some green boughs over the body, so that the dirt wouldn't tetch it, and filled it up easy-like and as gentle as I could. And when the fillin' was all in I went and cut some sod with my huntin' knife, with the flowers all growin' in them, and made the grave as green and pritty as natur could be and than I took position soldier-like and let off my piece as a kind of farewell and the hound lifted up his voice and gave one lament; and the sarvice was over."

Here the old man paused, and as I stirred the fire the flame leaped up and brought the features of his time-beaten face in clear relief. And a remarkable face it was, and such as is seldom given to man save when nature produces her noblest work. It may interest some who have been introduced to him in these pages and who will meet him further on in many scenes, both of peace and war, and who will grow to love him for the purity of his nature, and the courage of his conduct when exposed to temptation on the one hand and peril and death on the other, to have a pen portrait of one of the most noted characters that the latter part of the last century and the early half of the present one produced.

John Norton was, even in his seventieth year over six feet in height, but so symmetrical was his proportion in his physical stature that great as it was, it was neither awkward nor ungainly. Temperate in his habits, and constant in the exercises which develop and retain muscular power, he was even at the time of our story a marvel of physical strength. But for the fact that his eye may have lost a trifle of its earlier brightness, and that his hair once black as a raven's wing was now sprinkled with threads of gray, it would have been impossible to believe he had reached the period of threescore years and ten, for his form was still erect, his step elastic and his voice clear and strong. His face was of that square, strong shape, such as you see in a few of the older men still living in New England but who are fast passing away, and with them we fear the type of self-reliant and indomitable character they represent. His eyebrows were large and abundant, and projected over the eyes. The eyes themselves were gray and changeful in color according to the method of the speaker. His nose was large, and straight and full at the nostrils and broad at the base. His mouth was firm and in a marked manner suggestive of power. His chin was round and handsome. Into this noble and remarkable countenance time had channeled many a line, and the years had spread the repose of age without weakening the aspect of determined strength. In color the skin was of course bronzed, but of so pure a tan that the blood showed almost as plainly as in an untanned countenance. And, as he sat at the close of his narrative gazing into the fire with his face almost solemn in the gravity of its expression I said to myself as I gazed steadily at it, revealed in its every line and wrinkle as it was by the clear blaze, "I have never seen so noble and remarkable a countenance among men." I grew to love it in subsequent years as a son loves the face of a father in whom is no guile.

At last he started from his revery and said, "Henry, the morn is comin', for I feel the changes in the air that tell the beginnin' of day. Let us heave the rest of the logs on the fire and stretch ourselves for a nap, for natur' has her rights and must be dealt reasonably with. We will sleep now, and by and by I will show you the man's grave."

I did as he requested and then, stretched at full length on either side of the fire, we fell asleep.

The sun was high in the heaven before I awoke. I rubbed my eyes to make sure of my sight as I started up, for breakfast was ready, and the Old Trapper sat on the log patiently waiting my waking. The old man divined my thought, for he said: "Nay, nay, Henry, you need not feel hurt because I got the start of ye; for sleep to the young is sweet, and I could not wake ye till natur' was satisfied. But the eyelids of the old rest lightly on their balls, and the rays of the sun wakes me quicker nor a bugler's note rouses a soger. So me and the hound have been stirrin' about, and between your pack and mine we have got a meal fit for a king. So jest take a dip in the lake off that rock there, and we will try the vartue of the victals."

After breakfast was over, the Old Trapper said, "Come, Henry, we will go to the grave, and I will show ye where the body of an unhappy man lies buried. I warrant the hound remembers the spot as well as I do."

A few minutes brought us to the point where we landed. The hound being in the bow of the boat, had touched the shore first, and mounted the bank. No sooner had he reached the top than he lifted his nose into the air, turned around once in his tracks as a hound will when searching for knowledge, then started in a straight line for the bluff.

"Aye, aye, I know'd the dog would recollect the spot," said the Trapper, "and there he goes on a trail that's been whitened by the snows of 'leven winters as if he was arter a buck jest started from his nest in the moss. It's sartinly wouderful what sense the Lord has given to his creturs, sech as the beaver and the dog, and even a wolf in the darkest night can tell the toe from the heel of a track, and I have seen the wild bosses on the prairies act as sarcumspect as if they was reasonin' mortals."

At this point the long, solemn cry of the hound rose into the air and rolled in mournful cadence over the lake. The Old Trapper halted a moment, and then as he turned toward me, he said:—

"You see Henry, the heart of the dog is true to his memory of the spot. I have heerd many a dog give vent to his grief over the grave of his master, long years arter it was made, and it should larn us mortals to be true to what we have promised the dead, and keep their graves green and sweet arter they have gone. Henry, I feel a leetle oneasy lest somethin' of ill has happened to the corpse on the bluff. Come, let us go and see."

So saying, he started for the knoll, and I followed on. We soon reached the upper edge, and the grave, with the hound sitting on his haunches at the foot of it, was before us. The Old Trapper's face brightened as he saw it had not been disturbed, for, except that the mound had shrunken somewhat, and that the green growths of nature were more luxuriant, it was evidently the same as when it had been fashioned eleven years before.

The Old Trapper paused as he reached the head of the mound, and leaning on the muzzle of his rifle, said, "Henry, the Lord has sartinly been marciful, and kept the grave ondistarbed, and natur' has made it handsomer than it was when me and the hound left it; and a sightly spot it is, and a cheerful one for a grave to be in, for the view up the lake is a good un, as ye see, Henry, and the pines overhead keep up a pleasant sort of a darge. Yis, it sartinly is a cheerful spot for a grave, and if me and the hound could make it seem reasonable to us we would sartinly pick some sech spot as this to lie in arter we are dead; but it don't square with our notions of right and wrong, and we can't make it nohow, though we have held many a council over it. Still, a grave makes solemn and instructive company for a mortal, especially for one as old as me and the hound; and it may be, a leetle overhaulin' the pack, and goin' over the count of the years we have lived sence we left this grave, wouldn't do either of us any hurt; and as it is a matter that the young and them that has long life ahead of them aint much interested in, perhaps it may be as well that ye go back to the camp and pack things up for a start, Henry, for we will take to the boats when me and the hound has done with our meditations."

Appreciating the wish of the Old Trapper to be for a brief time alone, I retired down the knoll, and entering the boat was soon at the camp. As I stepped ashore, I cast my eyes across the bay to the bluff, and then I uncovered my head. The Old Trapper, with the hound looking steadily into his upturned face, was kneeling at the head of the grave, engaged in prayer.

5

QUEEN OF THE SNOW

I.

"I am Queen of the Snow, of the pure white snow.
I eddy and circle and whirl as I go.
I am Child of the Frost. I am born above mountains;
I mantle the forest; I cover the fountains.
I waver and fall, I stream and I flow,
With the currents of wind. I am beautiful snow!

CHORUS.

"She is Queen of the Snow, of the pure white snow.
We flakes are her subjects: we whirl as we go;
We eddy and circle; we stream and we flow.
She is Child of the Frost. She is beautiful snow!

II.

"When flowers are all withered, and their fragrance is fled;
When the wild grape is fallen, and the green leaf is dead;
When out of the forest the song-birds are flown,
And the harvest is reaped from the seed that was sown;
Then, then, from the sky to the earth far below
I come down in mercy. I am beautiful snow.

CHORUS.

"When flowers are all withered, and their fragrance is fled;
When the wild grape is fallen, and the green leaf is dead;
Then, then, from the sky to the earth far below
She comes down in mercy. She is beautiful snow!"

6

HENRY HERBERT'S THANKSGIVING

"I wish to heaven John Norton and the Lad were here!"

Those were the words that were said.

A large room, long, wide, and lofty as to its ceiling. A room builded by wealth. A room furnished with taste and yet extravagantly; in which the semi-barbaric and the effeminate stood in strange conjunction. From the horns of an elk that stretched widely above the doorway, hung vases of flowers and delicate vines that trailed their green sprangles over the savage prongs. A bison's head with its shaggy frontal, bead-like, glistening eyes, stout horns, and the red froth dropping from his half-open mouth was framed against the wall above the mantel. A pair of lavender gloves had been tossed upward and lay in the shaggy hair that curled above the roots of the horns. The floor was of oak, polished and waxed. Here and there costly rugs, with brave scenery woven in: Hounds in full career on one; two knights in full tilt, with splintered lances—one reeling from the saddle, on another. An Indian, feathered like a chief, cautiously picking up a trail, blazoned on a third. Brackets for guns everywhere. Foils, swords, boxing gloves, pistols; some ancient weapons, curiously wrought, lying on shelves and hanging from hooks of polished steel, ivory-tipped, driven into the wall. Beneath the bison's head above the mantel, on a set of red deer's antlers, lay a double rifle, and by it a paddle, with a huge glengorm stone set into the handle knob. A table covered with food and fruit and flowers—a table with four plates, and a man at the head of the table. He had been eating. Perhaps he had finished the meal. Perhaps he had stopped in the midst of it. Be that as it may, the man lifted his eyes to the double rifle resting on the deer's antlers, and at the paddle in which the stone was blazing; gazed at them as one gazes when his eyes are full of memories. And then, as he lowered his eyes to the table, and his head drooped slightly forward, said:

"I wish to heaven John Norton and the Lad were here!"

A noise outside the door; a noise in the great hall beyond; a noise of feet that brushed along and fell lightly; a noise of dogs rushing forward and held stoutly back; a noise of servants' voices expostulating, ejaculating, directing. A noise that moved, came on,—and as the great door swung open, burst with clatter and tumult into the room.

"John Norton!"

It was a shout;—a shout that burst into the air as a bomb explodes; a shout that bore the heart out of the mouth with it; a shout that plucked the body up from out the chair, planted it on its feet, and sent it with a mighty leap toward the open door, the struggling hounds, and the great broad-chested man that stood braced, holding them back; a shout that man gives but seldom, and never save when heart and soul go out in such welcome as a friend receives when he comes unexpectedly into a comrade's presence that was longing for him.

"John Norton!"

"Sartin, boy, sartin," said the Trapper. "That's my name for sartin;" and his great face glowed and beamed as he shook the other's hand. "Yis, here be me and the pups; and of ye'll look jest by the door post there, ye'll see somebody else."

As he spoke a tall, slim form stepped forward from the shadow of the door in which it had been standing, and a long, thin hand at the end of a long thin arm met the palm swept out to receive it: and so Herbert and the Trapper and the Lad met in Herbert's house on Thanksgiving night.

So these three men stood looking as they held each other's hands—looking at each other. Perhaps they said something, perhaps they didn't. If they did speak I doubt if they knew it. Strong men, steady and self-poised. Men trained as to the nerves, either of whom could die in such a fashion as to make the other two prouder of him than if he had lived. Men who loved each other beyond the love of woman. So they stood holding each other's hands looking at each other.

"Henry," said the Trapper at length, "the pups has come fur to see ye. We musn't be selfish in our greetin'. They be well-mannered, but a word from ye and a tech of yer hand will fetch the heart from atween their ribs."

That sentence broke the silence—broke the quiet and charm of it,—and in an instant Herbert was with the dogs, or rather the dogs were on Herbert: their paws on his shoulder; their tongues on his face, and his arms around their bodies hugging them. And then down the three went on to the rug,—the rug on which he had had their pictures woven in bright colors—playing with them; playing with abandon, as a hunter plays with his dogs when dogs and man are in frolicsome mood. What feints he made at them; what dashes they at him! What crouchings and leaps; and then the tumble in a heap, while the man's voice in laughter and the dogs' deep bayings rose and swelled till the air of the room vibrated to the ceiling.

"Hi, pups! hi, pups!" called the Trapper who stood himself laughing at the boisterous play. "Hi, pups, away with yer nonsense, and git ye up from the floor, boy; yer mats aint skins, and ye'll have them in threads ef ye aint keerful. Lord, how the pups will dream of this, when they're back in the cabin, and the wind storms over the chimney', and they lie quiverin' in their gladness as their memories work when they be asleep on their hearthstun."

The dogs obeyed the call of their master and seated themselves on their haunches demurely in outward appearance, but with eyes still glistening. The Trapper stood and scanned the room. He looked at the pictures on the wall, the stretch of the antlers, the bison's head, the double gun and the paddle. He looked at the polished floor, the blazoned rugs, and then at the table bright with dishes such as his eyes had never beheld: looked as a man looks with eyes trained to note the minutest thing and take the parts and the whole all in at a glance, and then he turned his eyes upon the young man and said:

"And this is yer cabin, boy?"

"Yes," answered Herbert. "This is my cabin, old friend; mine and yours and the Lad's."

"It be well said, boy," answered the Trapper; "yis it be well said. It be different from mine, but the heart and the greetin' makes it the same." And he looked at Herbert with eyes that brimmed, and added, as if speaking to himself, but half turning to the lad, "it be different than ourn, but the heart and the greetin', Lad, makes it the same."

"I'm glad you have come just as you have," said Herbert, "for I was on the point of eating my Thanksgiving dinner. The table is spread, you see, and the dishes are ready."

"Ye don't mean to say, boy, that ye cooked all these things yerself?" asked the Trapper, as he looked at the dozen and one preparations under which the table fairly groaned.

"No," answered Herbert, "I didn't. In the cities we have cooks that cook for us; for we are too busy to do our own cooking."

"Hoot, boy," answered the Trapper, "ye be sartinly off the trail, there. I can't conceit that a man can be too busy to cook his own vittals; for when he cooks his own vittals, he cooks 'em for his own mouth, and it makes safe eatin'. I trust yer cook, as ye call him, boy, is a man that can be trusted."

"My cook," answered Herbert, "is a woman. We have very few men cooks in the city."

"I dunno, I dunno," said the Trapper incredulously, "it may be safe cookin' as ye say; but I never knowed a squaw, or a white woman either, that a man that was at all tasty could trust in the matter of his vittals, unless it was in the makin' of pies and cake and sech leetle things that don't stay in a man's stomach half long enough, or else stay in his stomach a good deal too long. I eat a pie up here at a shanty on the Connecticut that has stayed with me ever sence, and the longer it stays the heavier it gits, and the pressure be a good deal like the gripes. I hadn't more'n got it down afore I knowed it wasn't honest cookin', and I gin the woman that peddled it to me, a piece of my mind. The Lad said she wasn't to blame, and it may be she wasn't; but that don't make any difference with a man with a stun in his stomach. Somebody is to blame, and I took a lick at the fust one that I could fasten it on; and I told the Lad—for he argued the p'int with me like a missioner—I told the Lad that ef I hadn't got the right un the Lord would see to that. But ef ye say the cookin' is honest, Henry, I'll believe ye, for ye know what good cookin' is, especially in the matter of meats; for I edicated ye myself." So saying, the old man proceeded toward the table and prepared to seat himself.

"Not there, not there!" exclaimed Herbert, "your place is at the head of the table. Take the chair at the head of the table, old friend. The house and the table and all you see, are yours. You are the father and we are the boys."

"The cabin sartinly looks as ef it was well built," answered the Trapper, as he looked at the solid oak walls, "and I don't doubt it will stand a good blow. The table is a big un and the vittals plenty. It may be that the cookin' is honest; ef ye say it is, it is, but I sartinly have doubts of the woman. But as to my takin' the head of the table, boy, that be another thing, and I conceit it isn't right, for the man that owns the cabin owns the table in it, and them that come to the table be his guests, and the place of honor be his, for he sarves them, and it be sarvin' that makes honor. Yis, boy, it be sarvin' that makes honor. And there be another p'int: ye've called me father, and ye say that the Lad and ye be boys; and the white in my head and the feelin' of my sperit towards ye make it fit that the word should be as ye said it, for all the young be boys and girls to the old; and the old be fathers and mothers to all the young ef their sperit be right. But a father loves to see his boy iu the place of honor, and I've come on a long trail, boy, to see ye in yer own cabin and at yer own table; and I'd rather sit furder down and see ye at the head of the table, Henry; for then I shall see what I've come fur to see—see ye in yer own cabin, at yer own table, and in the seat of honor. For there is no place so honorable," said the old man, speaking with true majesty of utterance, "there is no place so honorable for a man to be seated, as in his own cabin, at the head of his own table, with his family and friends ranged round him, on Thanksgivin' Day, when with feastin' and merriment he keeps the good old custom up."

"Henry," said the Trapper, as they all seated themselves at the table, "I ax yer pardin ef I be sayin' anything agin manners, but there be one plate too many or else there be one eater too few. The cabins be thick hereabouts, and down in the swale to the north-east, as the Lad and me come up along the line of the blazin', I seed a good many standin' round that looked to me as of they'd. been stand in' round, a good, while; and I told the Lad that I didn't understand why they looked so gant. and why they wasn't in their cabins overseein' the cookin.'"

"I doubt if some of them you saw, John Norton, had any houses at all, or"—

"No housen, boy," interrupted the Trapper; "why, the housens be thicker down in the swale there than fur on a beaver's pelt; and they have actually growed out over the trail, some of 'em, as ef they would shet the very sky from the sight of the trail underneath. Ye don't mean to tell me, boy, that there be any people in this settlement without housen, do ye?"

"There are certainly many, John Norton, not only without houses, but who haven't a place to lay their head, unless it be in the open street."

"God of marcy, Henry!" exclaimed the Trapper, "do ye mean to say that there is a man in this settlement to-day that hasn't a Thanksgivin' table to go to, or that there is a man that has no better place to sleep than the stuns of the paved carries? Why, boy, they be colder than a coffin."

"I am sorry to say, John Norton," answered the young man, "that the facts are as I have stated."

"Henry," replied the Trapper, as he rose from his chair, "there be a man standin' down in the swale over here beside an elm with a cracked trunk and an iron band round it; leastwise, he was standin' there when me and the Lad come by,—that looked as ef he had been lost in the woods for a month, and had lived on the memory of vittals he had eat when a boy, for his face was pinched and the place where ye tighten the belt looked holler. Ef ye've no objection I'll go down and fetch him up and set him by the plate there. The vittals will taste sweeter in our mouths ef the sweetness, as we eat, be in his'n. I see ye have a plenty, boy; and ef the meat should gin out and the woman be onsartin, I've got some jerked venison in my pack that I brought as a sort of a gift to ye, that'll stay by the man, ef he be reasonably good at swallerin', ontil he gets luck in his huntin'. Have ye got any objection, boy?"

"No, no, John Norton," replied the young man; "for God's sake, go and bring him in. It shan't be said that a man goes hungry to-day, if he can come to my house; and I'm ashamed, old friend, that I myself haven't found him—and not you."

"It is all in the eye, boy," answered the Trapper; "yis, it be all in the eye. Yer eye gits keen in the woods; but the settlements blind ye. He stood in the shadder of the tree, pinched up agin the bark; but I noted him, and his look was the look of a starvin' man. I'll have him here in a minute. He's there yit, I'll warrant; for he looked a good deal like an icicle that's froze to the bark."

"You had better let me go with you, John Norton," answered Herbert; "the streets are very narrow and crooked, and I am afraid you won't find him."

"Henry," said the Trapper, as he paused in the doorway, "Ye be forgitful. Yer trails be a good deal mixed, and the Lord only knows how they come to cross each other so often; but I took the p'ints of the compass as I ris the hill, and I'll go as straight to the man as a bee steers for his hole,—leastwise, as straight as a bee could ef he had to foller the onreasonable crookedness of yer trails here."

So saying, the Trapper disappeared. But the door opened the next instant, and the head of the Trapper re-appeared, and he said:

"Henry, ye might as well speak a word to the man that keeps the door of the cabin, for he was a leetle sassy to me and the Lad when we knocked for entrance; and I shouldn't stop to argue the p'int with him the next time. So it may be ye'd better speak to the vagabond to save any onpleasantness when I come back. I sartinly don't want any foolin' at the door of yer cabin."

Ten minutes passed—fifteen—twenty—and the Trapper came—came not alone; but with him another, and that other—well, we will describe him:

Age, thirty-five. Not a day older; at least his looks did not show it. In stature of medium height,—five feet ten, perhaps,—hair brown, eyes gray, nose straight, mouth a trifle too small, face clean shaven, though the beard was beginning to roughen it, hollow cheeks, darkish rims round the eyes, and at the corners of the mouth wrinkles that stretched downward: wrinkles that seemed about to become permanent lines. The superficial expression of that face was that of hunger. Back of that, like a man lying in wait, watching to strike, watching and waiting, was a dogged look; the look of a man who has borne all he could stand and has come nigh to that point in which he will stand it no longer.

"Here be the man, Henry," said the Trapper. "I found him by the elm, as I told ye. He'll pardin an old man's sayin' so, but I found him a leetle cross, and I may say a leetle onsartin techin' my sperit. And when I told him that I'd come with an invite to a

Thanksgivin' party, the man said I lied. I didn't arger the p'int with him; leastwise not as I might in some sarcumstances. But I got him out of the shadder of the elm, under a candle that stood in a box, and barnt without any wick to it, and I axed him to look at my face; and then we convarsed a leetle more. I told him where I'd come from and what my name was; and I told him I conceited that he'd been on a poor line and his trappin' hadn't paid; and he said the trap he'd been on hadn't paid, and was a leetle luny-like, as I conceited, in his head. But I told him it didn't matter, ef his stomach was right; and arter a leetle more talk he agreed to come along with me. He fetched the carry a leetle weakly; but here he is at last, and ef I'm any jedge of looks, he'll help us out in the eatin' a good deal, even ef the cook be a woman. And now, friend," said he, looking at the man, "what be yer name, and what shall we call ye?"

During the conversation of the Trapper, the man had evidently taken the measure of Herbert and the Lad; for he had looked at both searchingly, with the least bit of defiance in his eyes, buttoning his coat a little closer round the throat as he looked. Perhaps he had a vest under it, perhaps a shirt under the vest; but either point was problematical. When the button nearest the throat was fixed he had busied himself in trying to pull down the sleeves of his coat, that were at least a couple of inches too short. This he had done slyly, as if not to attract attention; and it was pitiful to see the thin fingers plucking at them. And when the Trapper asked what his name might be he looked him full in the face for an instant and said:

"James Munroe."

"James," said the old man, "I be, as I told ye, but a trapper. The boy that sets at the side of the table be my companion; and the boy that sets at the head of the table be Henry—Henry Herbert. He owns this cabin, and the Lad and me have come down from the woods to eat Thanksgivin' with him; and we got in jest in time, for we found the vittals on the table and everything ready. Ye see, there be only three of us and I noted there was four plates. Ye see, Henry has camped a good deal with me and the Lad, and he's often axed us to come down, and so we come; yis, we ambushed him, as it was, for he sartinly didn't know we was comin'. But ye see, he had three plates besides his own, and I conceit that he was thinkin' of us and so't the two plates for me and the Lad, and the other plate he sot for the stranger that should come. For the boy's heart be a good un, and he knows that them that be rich should have one plate for themselves and one plate for them that be poor. And as I looked at the plate I thought of ye, and the boy told me to go and fetch ye, and we four would eat Thanksgivin' together. Now, as I have told ye all there is to tell, and who we be, there is no reason why we shouldn't sot down and begin." And the Trapper moved towards his chair.

But the man never moved, but stood in his tracks looking first at one and then at the other, then at the table, and then at the chair in front of the plate that the Trapper had told him was set for him.

"Come, hist along," said the Trapper to him, speaking in a cheerful voice, "hist along toward yer chair. The cookin' was done by a woman, but Henry says it be honest, and the vittals be plenty; and I sartinly be empty, and ye don't look actally full yerself. Hist along friend, and we'll begin."

But the man still kept his tracks, and moved not an inch, but looked at the Trapper, at Herbert and the Lad, at the table and the plate with incredulous eyes.

"Old man, are you fooling me?"

It was all he said; but oh! with what emphasis he said it, and what a look there was in his eyes as he said it! And his fingers, how they shut into his palms and how his mouth twitched!

"Friend," said the Trapper, and he rose from the chair in which he had seated himself, "I have never lived in the settlements, and I know not what tricks men play on each other where the cabins of the rich and the shanties of the poor stand so nigh together. But I've lived in the woods where the rich and poor be alike; fur natur feeds one as highly as another, and clothes them as warmly; and in the woods we say what we mean, and we act as we feel. The boy has consorted with us and ketched our ways, and his heart be right by natur; and though I be in his cabin and not mine, and though this be his table and not mine, and though I've not cooked these vittals myself, yit"—the old man paused a moment, and lifting one hand to his head already so nearly white, he laid his palm on his gray locks and said, "friend, look at my head; then look at my face, and there be my hand. Do I look like a man that would lie? I say ye be welcome. Do I look like a man that would fool ye? I say this be yer table as truly as ourn; fur this be Thanksgivin' day, and Thanksgivin' day is for them that be poor and them that be hungry, and we be yer brothers. Sit down."

What is that strange quality in some that can make their saying simple words sound so nobly? Is it in the voice; the face; the bearing? or doth the quality of nobleness spring into life from the centre of the soul itself? Or is it that some are gifted to pour their best self out in speech, and make the words glow like a divine translation of themselves? We know not. But no one would dream, reading the plain simple words that he spoke to the ill-clad, hungry, starving man in front of him, how nobly they sounded in the speaking.

And so the feast began. The four were hungry, and they ate like hungry men. The man at the foot of the table ate as one who is starving, but whose good breeding restrained his eating from becoming ravenous. As the feasting proceeded the Trapper's tongue was loosened in speech, and the quaint humor, the sly wit, and the touches of true eloquence which characterized him, flowed out of him as a brook in spring-time flows through the meadows, now wimpling slyly underneath the trailing reeds, now breaking noisily down a little flight of rapids.

"Henry," said the Trapper, "yer woman be a good un. The partridge sartinly be a leetle dry, but the goose be cooked to a turn. Friend," said the Trapper, turning to the man, "will ye divide the rest of the goose with me?"

"No," said the man, pleasantly, "I've eaten enough. It has been years since I have had such a feast." Then he added, speaking soberly, "It may be years before I have another."

"I don't understand ye," said the Trapper, "ye be an able-bodied man, and work brings money, and money buys feastin'."

By this time the dinner had been amply discussed, and the chair of each, by a common involuntary movement, had been slightly moved back from the table. The conversational period had come, and each was ready to listen.

"Yes," answered the man, "money buys feasting, and labor and work earn money; but what is a man to do if he can get no work, John Norton?"

"The world be full of work," answered the Trapper. "Ye don't say that ye can find no work, friend?"

"Perhaps," answered the man, "a brief sketch of my life and some of the experiences of it, may help entertain you. As I look into your faces and recall your honorable and generous treatment, I am moved to open my heart to you. The bitterness that was in it when I entered the room is gone. The world I was ready to curse, you have taught me, by your kindness, to bless. Shall I tell you my story, gentlemen?"

"Sartin, friend, sartin; leastwise, ef ye feel like tellin' it. We was strangers to ye, but them that eat together be no longer strangers. Wherever they meet they be friends. Yis, tell us yer story, and tell it as ef ye was tellin' it to friends."

The man paused a moment as if to collect his thoughts, and then said:

"I was born in this city. My family was a wealthy and honored one. I trace my ancestry to the earliest settlers. The name I have given you is not my true name. I assumed it to hide my shame. Can you guess, old man, whom you are looking at?"

"Who be I lookin' at?" queried the Trapper.

"You are looking at *a criminal*, sir," said the man.

"Did ye break the laws?" asked the Trapper.

"I did," answered the man.

"What law did ye break, friend?" again asked the Trapper.

"I stole," answered the man. "Gentlemen, you have entertained a thief," and he spoke half doggedly.

"Thieves be hungry," said the Trapper, "and Thanksgivin' Day be for the hungry."

"I thank you for your charity," responded the man, "I shall remember you old man, when some other man with less charity shuts the door in my face when I, because I am starving, go to ask bread that I may not steal."

"Tut, tut," said the Trapper, "ye might work."

"I stole, as I told you," said the man, "I stole as gentlemen steal, not like a common thief. I wrote another man's name on a bit of paper. They call it forgery in the cities. Mr. Herbert there understands it. My forgery was detected. I was arrested. I was tried and condemned. I was sentenced to prison. It was just. My heart admitted the justice of the sentence, and I swear to you that

I went to my prison joyfully. I said, I will work my sentence out. I will pay the claim in full. I will come forth a man, and as a man I will start life again."

"That's right," said the Trapper; "a good many of us have started ag'in, off and on, and the Lord of marcy is never tired in givin' a man a new start, as I jedge."

"He may not be," answered the man, "but man is, and society is. Society never gives a man or a woman a new start."

"That's wrong," said the Trapper.

"It may be," answered the man; "but it is true. I have tried it, and know. I served my sentence out. I came out of prison. I changed my name that the memory of my disgrace might not stand in my way. I searched for employment: I obtained it. I served my employers faithfully. I rose in their esteem. By faithful attendance to my duty they grew to trust me. My future was bright, when one day I was called into the presence of the firm. They asked me if I had been in prison. I told them I had. They said they should be obliged to discharge me. I pleaded with them. I asked them if I had not served them well? if I had not been faithful? if I was not serviceable? They admitted all; but they said I must go."

"It wasn't right," said the Trapper.

"No," answered the man, "it wasn't right; but that made no difference,—I went. I searched for another place. The same fate met me there. I went to a third place. Two months ago I was discharged from that,—discharged not because I had not done my duty; not because I could not serve them well;—not because of any fault they found with me, but simply because I had been in prison. I could not beg. I swore to God I would not steal. I had but little money; and I made it last as long as I could; but—"

The man paused a moment, and then unbuttoning his coat at the throat, he pulled it apart,—pulled it apart with a quick, sudden motion; and then the three saw that the only garment that covered his shoulders and chest was the coat, old and thin. He said, as he rose from the chair:

"Gentlemen, look here. Is this the way for society that calls itself Christian; that calls itself just; that calls itself charitable and forgiving, to treat a man,—a man born in this city, educated in its schools, with an ancestry that goes back to the Mayflower,— because he has done one misdeed, when he has borne his sentence bravely, and as bravely set to work to rebuild his life? Is this the way to treat a man," he reiterated with rising voice,—"refusing him work when work means money and money means clothing and bread, and leave him standing on her streets, shivering in the cold and dying of starvation on Thanksgiving Day,—the day when Christian bells are ringing, and the tables in every house are loaded with food? Mr. Herbert, what do you say when society treats a man like that?"

Mr. Herbert, sitting at the head of the table jumped to his feet, stirred to quickest motion by the energy of the stranger's appeal; jumped to his feet and exclaimed! or would have exclaimed! but as he looked he could neither see *the man, nor the Trapper, nor the Lad!* They had disappeared! He looked for the dogs, but they too were gone! There was the table at which he had seated himself to eat his Thanksgiving dinner; the four plates; his own showing evidence of having been used; but the other three clean and white as when the servant had laid the cloth!

He sank back into his chair with a bewildered look on his face. Gradually it passed away, and he returned fully to his waking senses. He lifted his eyes to the double rifle that rested on the antlers of the red deer, and at the paddle with the Glengorm stone blazing in its shaft, balanced beneath it, and said:

"Strange that a dream could be so real." And then after a moment's pause he added,

"I wish to heaven, John Norton and the Lad were here."

7

THE BALL

"And his the music to whose tone
The common pulse of man keeps time,
In cot or castle, mirth or moan,
In cold or sunny clime."

—*Halleck.*

It was evening—dark, cool and starry. The earth and water lay hidden in the dusky gloom. Above, the stars were at their brightest. They gleamed and glowed, flashed and scintillated, like jewels fresh from the case. Their fires were many-colored—orange, yellow and red; and here and there a great diamond fastened into the zone of night, sent out its intense, colorless brilliancy. Through all the air silence reigned. The winds had died away, and the waters had settled to repose. No gurgle along the shore; no splash against the great logs that made the wharf; no bird of night calling to its mate. Outside all was still. Nature had drawn the curtains around her couch, and, screened from sight, lay in profound repose.

Within all was light, and bustle, and gayety. From every window lights streamed and flashed. The large parlors were alive with moving forms. The piano, whose white keys were swept by whiter hands, tinkled and rang in liveliest measure. The dance was at its height; and the very floor seemed vibrant with the pressure of lively feet. The dancers advanced, retired, wheeled and swayed in easy circles, swept up and down, and across the floor in graceful lines.

Amid the happy scene the Old Trapper stood, his stalwart frame erect as in his prime; while his great strong face fairly beamed in benediction upon the dancers. For his nature had within its depths that fine capacity which enabled it to receive the brightness of surrounding happiness and reflect it again.

It was a study to watch his face, and mark the passage of his changeful moods: surprise, delight, and broad, warm-hearted humor, as they came to and played across the responsive features. The man of the woods, of the lonely shore, and of silence, seemed perfectly at home amid the noise and commotion of human merry-making.

At last the music died away. The dancers checked their feet. The lady who had been playing the piano rose wearily from the instrument and joined a group of friends. The music was not adequate. The notes were too sharp; too isolate; they did not flow together. There was no sweep and swing, nor suavity of connected progress in the strains. The instrument could not lift the dancers up and swing them onward through the mazy motions.

"I tell ye, Henry," said the Old Trapper, as he turned to Herbert who was standing by his side, "the pianer isn't the thing to dance by, for sartin. It tinkles and chippers too much; it rattles and clicks. It don't git hold of the feelin's, Henry;—it don't start the blood in yer veins, nor set yer skin tinglin', nor make the feet dance agin yer will. It's good enough in it's way, no doubt; but it sartinly isn't the thing to lift the young folks up and swing 'em round. The fiddle is the thing;—yis, the fiddle is sartinly the thing. I would give a good deal if we had a fiddle here to-night, for I see the boys and girls miss it. Lord-a-massy! how it would set 'em agoin' if we only had a fiddle here."

"John Norton," said the Lad, who was sitting on a chair hidden away behind the Trapper, "John Norton," and the Lad took hold of the sleeve of his jacket and pulled the Trapper's head down towards him, "would you like to hear a violin to-night?"

"Like to hear a fiddle? Lord bless ye Lad, I guess I would like to hear a fiddle. I never seed a time I wouldn't give the best beaver hide in the lodge to hear the squeak of the bow on the strings. What's the matter with ye, Lad! What makes ye look so, boy?"

Well might he ask the question, for the Lad's face was absolutely radiant. His eyes were glowing and his lips fairly apart as if with suppressed eagerness, the eagerness of restrained excitement.

"John Norton!" said the Lad, and he drew the old man's bead still closer to him until his ear was within a few inches of his mouth, "I love to play the violin better than I love anything in the world, and I've got one of the best ones, you ever heard, out there in the bow of the boat."

"Heavens and 'arth, Lad!" ejaculated the Trapper, "did ye say ye could play the fiddle, and that ye had a good one out there in the boat? Lord-a-massy! how the young folks will hop. Scoot out there and git it, boy, and Henry and me will let the folks know what ye've got and what ye can do."

The Lad fairly flashed out of the room. He was gone in an instant; and in a few minutes he had returned, bearing in his hands a bundle which he carried as carefully as a mother would carry her babe; but brief as had been his absence it had allowed sufficient time for Herbert to communicate with the master of ceremonies and for him to announce to the company present that the great lack of the occasion had fortunately and unexpectedly been supplied; for the young man who was with Mr. Herbert and John Norton not only knew how to play the violin but actually had one in his boat and had just gone to get it, and would be back in a moment. The announcement was received with applause. White hands clapped, and a hundred ejaculations of wonderment sounded forth the surprise and pleasure of the eager throng. And when the Lad came stealing in, bearing his precious burden, he was received with a positive ovation.

It was amusing to see the change which had come over the looks and actions of the company at the mention and appearance of the violin. The faces that had shown indifference and the look of languid weariness freshened and became tense in all their lines; and on their heads again animation sat crowned. Those who were seated jumped to their feet. The conversationalists broke their circle and swung suddenly into line. Eyes sparkled. Little happy screams and miniature war-whoops from the boisterous youngsters rang through the parlor. In eye, and look, and voice, the popular tribute spoke in honor of the popular instrument,—an instrument whose strings can sound almost every passion forth: The quip and quirk of merriment, the mourner's wail, the measured praise of solemn psalms, the lively beat of joy, the subtle charm of indolent moods, and the sweet ecstasy of youthful pleasure, when with flying feet and in the abandon of delight she swings, circles, and floats through the measures of the voluptuous waltz.

In one corner of the parlor there was a raised platform, from which charades and private theatricals had been acted on some previous evening, and to this the Lad was escorted; and strange to say his awkwardness had departed from him. His form was straight. His head raised. His shambling gait steadied itself with firmer confidence. His long arms sought no longer feebly to bide themselves, but held the package that he carried in fond authority of gesture, as a proud mother, whose pride had banished bashfuluess, might carry a beautiful child—a child that was her own. So the Lad went towards the raised dais, and seating himself in the chair, proceed with deliberate tenderness to uncover the instrument.

An old, dark-looking one it was. The gloom of centuries darkened it. Their dusk had penetrated the very fibres of the wood. Its look suggested ancient times; far climes; and hands long mouldering in dust. It was an instrument to quicken curiosity and elicit mental interrogation. What was its story? Where was it made? By whom, and when? The Lad did not know. It was his mother's gift, he said. And an old sea-captain had given it to his mother. The old sea-captain had found it on a wreck in the far-off Indian Ocean. He found it in a trunk—a great sea chest made of scented wood and banded with brazen ribs. And in the chest, with it, it was rumored were silks, and costly fabrics, and gold and eastern gems,—gems that never had been cut; but lay in all their barbaric beauty, dull and swarth as Cleopatra's face. Thus the violin had been found on the far seas—at the end of the world, as it were, and in companionship of gems and fabrics rich and rare; and in a chest whose mouth breathed odors. This was all the Lad knew.

"Henry," said the Old Trapper, "the Lad says the fiddle is so old that no one knows how old it is; and I conceit the boy speaks the truth. It sartinly looks as old as a squaw whose teeth has dropped out and whose eyes are half shet, and her face the color of tanned buckskin. I tell ye, Henry, I believe it will bust if the Lad draws the bow with any 'arnestness across it, for there never was a glue made that would hold wood together for a thousand year. And if that fiddle isn't a thousand year old, then John Norton is no jedge of appearances; and can't count the prongs on the horns of a buck."

At this instant the Lad dropped the bow on to the strings. Strong and round, mellow and sweet, the note swelled forth; starting with the least filament of sound, it wove itself into a compact chord of sonorous resonance; filled the great parlors; passed through the doorway into the receptive stillness outside; charged it with throbbings—thus held the air a moment; reigned in it—then, called its powers back to itself; drew in its vibrating tones; checked its undulating force; and leaving the air by easy retirement came back like a bird to its nest and died away within the recesses of the dark, melodious shell from whence it started.

When the bow first began its course across the strings the Old Trapper's eyes were on it; and as the note grew and swelled he seemed to grow with it. His great fingers shut into their palms as if an unseen power were pulling at the cords. His breast heaved full. His mouth actually opened. It was as if the rising, swelling, pulsating sounds lifted him from off the floor on which he stood; and when the magnificent note ebbed and finally died away within the violin, not only he, but all the company stood breathless: charmed, surprised, astonished into silence at the wondrous strain they had heard.

The Old Trapper was the first to move. He brought his brawny hand down heavily on to Herbert's shoulder and with a face actually on fire with the fervor stirred within him, exclaimed:—

"Lord-a-massy! Henry, did ye ever hear a noise like that? I say, boy, did ye ever hear a noise like that? Where on 'arth did it all come from? Why, boy, 'twas as long and as solemn as a funeral, as arnest as the cry of a panther; and roared like the nest of hornets when ye poke 'em up with a stick. If that's a fiddle I wonder what the other things be that I have heerd the half-breeds and the Frenchers play in the clearin's."

Well might the Old Trapper be astonished. The violin of unknown age and make was one among ten thousand. It was a concert to hear the Lad tune it; which he did with a bold and skillful touch, and the exactness of an ear which nature had made exquisitely true to time and chord. His bashfuluess was gone. His timidity had departed. His awkwardness, even, went out of body and arm and fingers, with the initial note. His soul had found its life with his mother's gift; and he who was so weak and hesitating in ordinary moments, found courage and strength, and the dignity of a master, when he touched the strings. At last the instrument was ready. And with a flourish bold and free he struck into the measures of a waltz that filled the parlor with a circling noise, and made the air throb and beat—swing and swell, as if it were liquid, and unseen hands were moving it with measured undulations.

There was no resisting an influence so sweet, subtle, and pervasive, as flowed from that easy-going bow, as it came and went over the resounding strings. Couple after couple swung off into the open space until the entire company were swinging and floating through the dreamy and bewitching measures. The god of music was actually in the room, and his strong, passionate touch was on the souls of those who were floated hither and thither as if blown by his invisible breath. The music actually took possession of the dancers. It banished the mortal heaviness from their frames, and made them buoyant so that their feet scarce touched the floor. Up and down and across, from side to side and end to end they whirled and floated. They moved as if a power which took the place of wings was in them. They did not seem to know that they were dancing. They did not dance; they floated; flowing like a current moved by easy undulations. Their hands were clasped. Their faces nearly touched. Their eyes were closed or glowing. And still the long bow came and went, and still the music rose and sank, and swelled and ebbed as easy waves advance, retreat and flood again, breaking in white and lazy murmurs at twilight on the dusky beach.

Herbert stood still; but his eyes were lifted, the gaze in them was far away, and one foot beat the measure. Beside him stood the Trapper. His arms were crossed; his eyes were on the bow that the Lad was drawing, and his body swayed, lifted and sank in perfect harmony with the motions and the accompanying sound, with a grace which nature only reaches when the will is utterly surrendered to a power that has charmed the stiffness and tension out of the frame and made it yielding and responsive.

At last the music stopped; and with it stopped each form. Each foot was arrested at the point to which the sound had carried it when it paused. Each couple stood in perfect pose. The motive power which moved them was withdrawn, and the limbs stood motionless as if the soul that gave them animation had retired. They had been lifted to another world—a world of impulse and movement more airy and spirit-like than the gross earth,—and it took a moment for them to struggle back to ordinary life. But in a moment thought recalled them to themselves, and they realized the mastery of the power that had held them at its will, and the applause broke out in showers of happy tumult. They crowded around the Lad—strong men and beautiful women,—gazing at him in wonder; then broke up into knots, talking and marveling. In the Old Trapper's face, as he gazed at the Lad, a strange look came,—the look of a man to whose soul has come a revelation so pure and sweet and clear that he is unable at first to compass it with his understanding. He came close to the Lad, and sitting down on the edge of the platform, put his hand on the knee of the youth, and said:—

"I have heerd most of the sweet and terrible noises that natur' makes, boy; I have heerd the thunder among the hills, when the Lord was knockin' agin the 'arth until it jarred; and I have heerd the wind in the pines and the waves on the beaches when the darkness of night was on the woods, and Natur' was singin' her evenin' psalm; and there be no bird or beast the Lord has made whose cry, be it lively or solemn, I have not heerd; and I have said that man had never made an insterment that could make so sweet a noise as Natur' makes when the Sperit of the univarse speaks through the stillness: but ye have made sounds to-night, Lad, sweeter than my ears have ever heerd on hill or lake-shore, at noon or in the night season, and I sartinly believe that the Sperit of the Lord has been with ye, boy, and gi'n ye the power to bring out sech music as the Book says the angels make in their happiness in the world above. I trust ye are grateful, Lad, for the gift the Lord has gi'n ye; for, though yer tongue knows leetle of speech, yit yer fingers can bring sech sounds out of that fiddle as a man might wish to have in his ears when his body lies in his cabin, and his sperit is standin' on the edge of the Great Clearin'. Yis, Lad, ye must sartinly play for me when my eyes grow dim, and my feet strike the trail that no man strikes but once, nor travels both ways."

At this point the announcement of supper was made; and the company streamed towards the tables. The repast was of that bounteous character customary to the houses located in the woods, in which the hearty provisions of the forest were brought into conjunction with and reinforced by the more light and fanciful *cuisine* of the cities. Among the substantials fish and venison predominated. There was venison roast and venison spitted and venison broiled, venison steak and venison pie. Trout broiled, and baked, and boiled; pancakes and rolls; ices and cream; pies and puddings; pickles and sauces of every conceivable character and make; ducks and partridges; coffee and tea whose nature, we regret to say, was discernible only to the eye of faith. In the midst of this abundance the Old Trapper was entirely at home. He ate with the relish and heartiness of a man whose appetite was of the highest order; and whose courage mounted to the occasion.

"I tell ye, Henry," said the old man, as he transferred a duck to his plate, and proceeded to carve it with the aptness of one who had practical knowledge of its anatomy, "I tell ye, Henry, the birds are gittin' fat; and I sartinly hope the flight this Fall will be a good 'un. Don't be bashful, Lad, in yer eatin'," he continued, as he transferred half of his bird to his companion's plate, "ye haven't got the size of some about the waist, but yer length is in yer favor and if ye will only straighten up, and Henry don't give out, there'll be leetle left on this eend of the table when we have satisfied our hunger. I don't know when the cravin' of natur' has been stronger within me than it is this minit, and if nothin' happens, and ye stand by me, the Saranacers will remember our visit for days arter we are gone. It isn't often that I feed in the settlements, or get a taste of their cookin', but the man who basted these birds knowed what he was doin', and the fire has given them jest the right tech; for the morsels actally melt in yer mouth."

The Trapper's feelings were evidently not peculiar to himself. For the spirit of feasting was abroad, and the eating was such as would astonish the dwellers in cities. Wit flashed across the table in answer to wit. Mirth rippled from end to end of the room. Laughter roared and rollicked adown the hall. Jokes were cracked. Fun exploded. Plates rattled. Cups and glasses touched and rang. Even the waiters as they came and went in their happy service caught the infection of the surrounding happiness and their laughter mingled with that of the guests.

The great pine branches and the evergreen nailed against the corner posts and wreathed into festoons along the walls shook and trembled in the uproar as to the passage of winds along their native hills. And the huge bucks' heads, whose antlers were tied with rosettes and streaming ribbons, lost the staring look of their great artificial eyes and seemed as they looked out through the interlacing boughs of cedar and balsam as if life had returned to them, and they once more were animate.

In about an hour the company streamed back into the parlor, with a mood even livelier than that which had characterized the early hours of the occasion. Their minds were in the state of highest action, and their bodies needed but the opportunity for rapid motion. Even the Lad had caught the infection of the surrounding liveliness, for his eyes and face glowed with the light of quickened animation.

"Have ye got any jigs in that fiddle, Lad," said the Trapper, "can ye twist anything out of yer instrument that will set the feet travelin'? It seems to me that the young folks here want shakin up a leetle; and a leetle of the old-fashioned dancin' will help 'em settle the victuals. Can ye liven up Lad, and give 'em a tune that will set 'em whirlin'.

The only reply of the Lad was a motion of the bow; but the motion was effective; for it sent a torrent of notes into the air, which thrilled through the body and tingled along the nerves like an electric shock. The Old Trapper fairly bounded into the air; and when he struck the floor his feet were flying. Nor was he alone; the jig had started a dozen on the instant; and the floor rattled and rang with the tap of toe and heel.

"Henry," said the Old Trapper, "hold on to me or I shall sartinly make a fool of myself. The Lad is ticklin' me from head to foot, and my toes are snappin' inside of the moccasins. Lord, who'd a thought that the blood in the veins of a man whose head is whitenin' could be sot leapin' as mine is doin' at this minit' by the scrapin' of a fiddle."

The Lad was a picture to see. His bow flew like lightning. His long fingers drummed and slid along the strings of the violin with bewildering swiftness. The little instrument jetted and effervesced its melody. The continuous and resounding noise poured out of it in tuneful bubbles. The air was full of tinkling fragments of sound. The Lad's body swayed to and fro. His face glowed. His eyes flashed. The sweat stood in drops on his forehead, but still the bow snapped and crinkled, and the instrument continued to burst in musical explosion, while the floor shook; the windows rattled; the lamps flared and fluttered, as the dancers chased the music on.

"Heavens and arth!" said the Trapper. "I can't stand this," and breaking from the hold that Herbert had on him he whirled himself out to the center of the floor, and with his face aflame with excitement, and his white hair flying abroad, he led the jig men off with the lightness of foot and rapidity of stroke that forced the music by half a beat. The effect was electric. The room burst with applause, and the Lad fetched a stroke that seemed to rip the violin asunder. It was now a race between the violin and the dancers. One after another fell out of the circle as the moments passed, until the Trapper was left alone and was cutting it down in a fashion that both astonished and convulsed the company. More than one of the spectators went on to the floor in paroxysms of laughter. Herbert, bent over with his hands on his knees, was watching the Trapper with mouth stretched to its utmost, and streaming eyes. The gambler was jumping up and down, utterly beside himself, calling for "odds."

It is impossible to say which would have triumphed, had not an accident decided the contest and brought the jig to an abrupt termination. For even while the Lad was in the midst of the swiftest execution, the hind legs of the chair in which he was sitting were whipped from their fastenings, his heels went into the air, and he turned half a somersault backward, and the music stopped with a snap.

It was minutes before a word could be heard. Roars and shrieks, and screams of irrepressible and uncontrolable merriment shook the house from foundation to garret. The Lad picked himself up, and for the first time since they met Herbert saw his placid countenance wrinkled and seamed with the contortions of uproarous mirth. The sluggishness of his temperament for once was thoroughly agitated, and the manhood which never before had come to the surface found in hilarity a visible and adequate expression. The Trapper had spun to his side and the two had joined their hands, and looking into each other's faces were laughing with a boisterousness that fairly shook their frames and exploded in resounding peals.

Gradually the uproar subsided, and the company settled by easy transition to a quieter mood. The hours of the night were

passing, and the moment drawing nigh when those who had mingled their merriment must part. The Old Trapper had regained his
gravity and his countenance had settled to its customary repose.
It seemed the general wish that the Lad should favor them with a
farewell piece, and, in compliance with the request of many, the
old man turned to him and said:—

"The hours be drawing on, Lad, and it's reasonable that we
should break up; but afore we go the folks wish to hear ye play
a quiet sort of a piece that may be cheerful and pleasant-like for
them to remember ye by when we be gone. So Lad if ye have got
anything in yer head that's soft and teching, somethin' that will
sort o' stay in the heart as the seasons come and go, I sartinly hope
ye will play it for them. And as ye say ye was born by the sea, and
as ye say the insterment ye hold in yer hand was gi'n ye by yer
mother, it may be ye can play us something our of yer memory
that shall tell us of her goodness to ye. Somethin', I mean, that
shall tell us of the shore where ye was born and the love that ye
had afore ye laid her to rest and came to the woods. Can ye play
us somethin' like that, Lad?"

"I can play you anything that has mother in it," said he, and a
wistful, yearning, hungry look came into his eyes, and the edges
of his simple lips quivered.

The company seated themselves, and the boy drew his bow
across the instrument. The brush of a painter could not have made
the picture more perfect, than the vision the Lad brought forth as
the bow played on the strings. The picture of a sea, sunlighted
and level, and stretching far out; the picture of a curved shore:
the shore of a quiet bay, rimmed with its beach of shining saud
and noisy with the gurgle and splash of lapsing waves; the picture
of a home quiet and orderly, and filled with the tenderness of a
gentle spirit; and then a heavier chord told of the coming of a
darker hour when the mother lay dying. The violin fairly sobbed
and groaned and wailed, as if the spirit of inconsolable grief were
tugging heavily at the strings. Anon, a bell tolled solemnly out
of it, and its heavy knell clanged through the room. And then the
music rested for a minute, and in the silence a grave came into
sight as plainly as if the eyes of all were actually looking at its
open mouth. Again the music sounded, and the sods, one after
another, fell on the coffin dull and heavy, changing to a smothered

sound as the grave filled. Once more it paused, and then a clear, sweet strain arose, sad, but pure, and fine, and hopeful, as voice of angels could have sung it, trustful and resigned. The bow stopped again; for a moment the violin was silent. And then the Lad lifted his face, and, laying the bow softly upon the strings, he began to play what all instinctively felt was a hymn to the spirit of his mother. Slowly, softly, sweetly as the strains which the dying sometimes hear, the pure, clear, smooth notes, stole out into the hushed air. It was playing, not such as mortal plays to mortal, but such as spirit might play to spirit, and soul to soul, across the street of heaven. The Lad still used an earthly instrument and touched its strings with mortal fingers; but never, while they live, will those who heard that hymn believe that anything less than the spirit of the boy;—as it shall be in mood when, in the spirit world, he first beholds his angel mother,—drew from the instrument the notes that filled that room with their divine sweetness. Indeed, the Lad did not act as if he were conscious of his body, or of bodily presences around him. His face was lifted, and his eyes, from which the tears were streaming, were gazing upward, not as if into vacancy, but as if they saw the bright being that had passed within the vail, but which now, for a moment, stood in all the beauty of her transfiguration before them. For a smile was on the boy's lips, even while the tears were rolling down his cheeks; and when, at last, the arm suspended its motion; when the sweet notes ceased to sound, and the last chord had died away, the Lad still kept his uplifted posture and his features held the same rapt expression.

The company sat motionless, their gaze fastened on the Lad. Not an eye was without its tear. The cheeks of the Old Trapper were wet; and Herbert, touched by some memory, or overcome by the pathos of the music, was actually sobbing. The old man, with a tread as light as a moccasined foot could make, stepped softly to the side of the Lad and taking him by the arm, while the company rose as one man, he motioned to Henry with his hand, and then, without a word, the Trapper, and Herbert, and "The Man Who Didn't Know Much," passed out of the room, and taking boat, shoved off and glided from sight in the blue darkness of the overhanging night, amid whose eastern gloom the great, luminous mellow-hearted stars of the morning were already aflame.

8

HOW JOHN NORTON THE TRAPPER KEPT HIS CHRISTMAS

JOHN NORTON THE TRAPPER.

I.

A CABIN. A cabin in the woods. In the cabin a great fireplace piled high with logs, fiercely ablaze. On either side of the broad hearth-stone a hound sat on his haunches, looking gravely, as only a hound in a meditative mood can, into the glowing fire. In the centre of the cabin, whose every nook and corner was bright with the ruddy firelight, stood a wooden table, strongly built and solid. At the table sat John Norton, poring over a book,—a book large of size, with wooden covers bound in leather, brown with age, and smooth as with the handling of many generations. The whitened head of the old man was bowed over the broad page, on which one hand rested, with the forefinger marking the sentence. A cabin in the woods filled with firelight, a table, a book, an old man studying the book. This was the scene on Christmas Eve. Outside, the earth was white with snow, and in the blue sky above the snow was the white moon.

"It says here," said the Trapper, speaking to himself, "it says here, 'Give to him that lacketh, and from him that hath not, withhold not thine hand.' It be a good sayin' fur sartin; and the world would be a good deal better off, as I conceit, ef the folks follered the sayin' a leetle more closely." And here the old man paused a moment, and, with his hand still resting on the page, and his forefinger still pointing at the sentence, seemed pondering what he had been reading. At last he broke the silence again, saying,—

"Yis, the world would be a good deal better off, ef the folks in it follered the sayin';" and then he added, "There's another spot in the book I'd orter look at to-night; it's a good ways furder on, but I guess I can find it. Henry says that the furder on you git in the book, the better it grows, and I conceit the boy may be right; for there be a good deal of murderin' and fightin' in the fore part of the book, that don't make pleasant readin', and what the Lord wanted to put it in fur is a good deal more than a man without book-larnin' can understand. Murderin' be murderin', whether it be in the Bible or out of the Bible; and puttin' it in the Bible, and sayin' it was done by the Lord's commandment, don't make it any better. And a good deal of the fightin' they did in the old time was sartinly without reason and ag'in jedgment, specially where they killed the women-folks and the leetle uns." And while the old man had thus been communicating with himself, touching the character of much of the Old Testament, he had been turning the leaves until he had reached the opening chapters of the New, and had come to the description of the Saviour's birth, and the angelic announcement of it on the earth. Here he paused, and began to read. He read as an old man unaccustomed to letters must read,—slowly and with a show of labor, but with perfect contentment as to his progress, and a brightening face.

"This isn't a trail a man can hurry on onless he spends a good deal of his time on it, or is careless about notin' the signs, fur the words be weighty, and a man must stop at each word, and look around awhile, in order to git all the meanin' out of 'em—yis, a man orter travel this trail a leetle slow, ef he wants to see all there is to see on it."

Then the old man began to read:—

"'Then there was with the angels a multitude of the heavenly host,'—the exact number isn't sot down here," he muttered; "but I conceit there may have been three or four hunderd,—'praisin' God and singin', Glory to God in the highest, and on 'arth, peace to men of good will.' That's right," said the Trapper. "Yis, peace to men of good will. That be the sort that desarve peace; the other kind orter stand their chances." And here the old man closed the book,—closed it slowly, and with the care we take of a treasured thing; closed it, fastened the clasps, and carried it to the great chest whence he had taken it, putting it away in its place. Having done this, he returned to his seat, and, moving the chair in front of the fire, he looked first at one hound, and then at the other, and said, "Pups, this be Christmas Eve, and I sartinly trust ye be grateful fur the comforts ye have."

He said this deliberately, as if addressing human companions. The two hounds turned their heads toward their master, looked placidly into his face, and wagged their tails.

"Yis, yis, I understand ye," said the Trapper. "Ye both be comfortable, and, I dare say, that arter yer way ye both be grateful, fur, next to eatin', a dog loves the heat, and ye be nigh enough to the logs to be toastin'. Yis, this be Christmas Eve," continued the old man, "and in the settlements the folks be gittin' ready their gifts. The young people be tyin' up the evergreens, and the leetle uns be onable to sleep because of their dreamin'. It's a pleasant pictur', and I sartinly wish I could see the merry-makin's, as Henry has told me of them, some time, but I trust it may be in his own house, and with his own children." With this pleasant remark, in respect to the one he loved so well, the old man lapsed into silence. But the peaceful contentment of his face, as the firelight revealed it, showed plainly that, though his lips moved not, his mind was still

active with pleasant thoughts of the one whose name he had men-
tioned, and whom he so fondly loved. At last a more sober look
came to his countenance,—a look of regret, of self-reproach, the
look of a man who remembers something he should not have forgotten,—and he said,—

"I ax the Lord to pardin me, that in the midst of my plenty I
have forgot them that may be in want. The shanty sartinly looked
open enough the last time I fetched the trail past the clearin', and
though with the help of the moss and the clay in the bank she
might make it comfortable, yit, ef the vagabond that be her husband has forgot his own, and desarted them, as Wild Bill said he
had, I doubt ef there be vict'als enough in the shanty to keep them
from starvin'. Yis, pups," said the old man, rising, "it'll be a good
tramp through the snow, but we'll go in the mornin', and see ef
the woman be in want. The boy himself said, when he stopped
at the shanty last summer, afore he went out, that he didn't see
how they was to git through the winter, and I reckon he left the
woman some money, by the way she follered him toward the boat;
and he told me to bear them in mind when the snow came, and
see to it they didn't suffer. I might as well git the pack-basket
out, and begin to put the things in't, fur it be a goodly distance,
and an early start will make the day pleasant to the woman and
the leetle uns, ef vict'als be scant in the cupboard. Yis, I'll git
the pack-basket out, and look round a leetle, and see what I can
find to take 'em. I don't conceit it'll make much of a show, fur
what might be good fur a man, won't be of sarvice to a woman;
and as fur the leetle uns, I don't know ef I've got a single thing
but vict'als that'll fit 'em. Lord! ef I was near the settlements, I
might swap a dozen skins fur jest what I wanted to give 'em; but
I'll git the basket out, and look round and see what I've got."

In a moment the great pack-basket had been placed in the middle of the floor, and the Trapper was busy overhauling his stores
to see what he could find that would make a fitting Christmas gift
for those he was to visit on the morrow. A canister of tea was first
deposited on the table, and, after he had smelled of it, and placed
a few grains of it on his tongue, like a connoisseur, he proceeded
to pour more than half of its contents into a little bark box, and,
having carefully tied the cover, he placed it in the basket.

"The yarb be of the best," said the old man, putting his nose to the mouth of the canister, and taking a long sniff before he inserted the stopple— "the yarb be of the best, fur the smell of it goes into the nose strong as mustard. That be good fur the woman fur sartin, and will cheer her sperits when she be down-hearted; fur a woman takes as naterally to tea as an otter to his slide, and I warrant it'll be an amazin' comfort to her, arter the day's work be over, more specially ef the work had been heavy, and gone sorter crosswise. Yis, the yarb be good fur a woman when things go crosswise, and the box'll be a great help to her many and many a night beyond doubt. The Lord sartinly had women in mind when he made the yarb, and a kindly feelin' fur their infarmities, and, I dare say, they be grateful accordin' to their knowledge."

A large cake of maple-sugar followed the tea into the basket, and a small chest of honey accompanied it.

"That's honest sweetenin'," remarked the Trapper with decided emphasis; "and that is more'n ye can say of the sugar of the settlements, leastwise ef a man can jedge by the stuff they peddle at the clearin'. The bees be no cheats; and a man who taps his own trees, and biles the runnin' into sugar under his own eye, knows what kind of sweetenin' he's gittin'. The woman won't find any sand in her teeth when she takes a bite from that loaf, or stirs a leetle of the honey in the cup she's steepin'."

Some salt and pepper were next added to the packages already in the basket. A sack of flour and another of Indian-meal followed. A generous round of pork, and a bag of jerked venison, that would balance a twenty-pound weight, at least, went into the pack. On these, several large-sized salmon-trout, that had been smoked by the Trapper's best skill, were laid. These offerings evidently exhausted the old man's resources, for, after looking round a while, and searching the cupboard from bottom to top, he returned to the basket, and contemplated it with satisfaction, indeed, yet with a face slightly shaded with disappointment.

"The vict'als be all right," he said, "fur there be enough to last 'em a month, and they needn't scrimp themselves either. But eatin' isn't all, and the leetle uns was nigh on to naked the last time I seed 'em; and the woman's dress, in spite of the patchin', looked as ef it would desart her, ef she didn't keep a close eye on't. Lord! Lord! what shall I do? fur there's room enough in the basket, and the woman and the leetle uns need garments; that is, it's more'n likely they do, and I haven't a garment in the cabin to take 'em."

"Hillo! Hillo! John Norton! John Norton! Hillo!" The voice came sharp and clear, cutting keenly through the frosty air and the cabin walls. "John Norton!"

"Wild Bill!" exclaimed the Trapper. "I sartinly hope the vagabond hasn't been a-drinkin'. His voice sounds as ef he was sober; but the chances be ag'in the signs, fur, ef he isn't drunk, the marcy of the Lord or the scarcity of liquor has kept him from it. I'll go to the door, and see what he wants. It's sartinly too cold to let a man stand in the holler long, whether he be sober or drunk;" with which remark the Trapper stepped to the door, and flung it open.

"What is it, Wild Bill? what is it?" he called. "Be ye drunk, or be ye sober, that ye stand there shoutin' in the cold with a log cabin within a dozen rods of ye?"

"Sober, John Norton, sober. Sober as a Moravian preacher at a funeral."

"Yer trappin' must have been mighty poor, then, Wild Bill, for the last month, or the Dutchman at the clearin' has watered his liquor by a wrong measure for once. But ef ye be sober, why do ye stand there whoopin' like an Indian, when the ambushment is onkivered and the bushes be alive with the knaves? Why don't ye come into the cabin, like a sensible man, ef ye be sober? The signs be ag'in ye, Wild Bill; yis, the signs be ag'in ye?'

"Come into the cabin!" retorted Bill. "An' so I would mighty lively, ef I could; but the load is heavy, and your path is as slippery as the plank over the creek at the Dutchman's, when I've two horns aboard."

"Load! What load have ye been draggin' through the woods?" exclaimed the Trapper. "Ye talk as ef my cabin was the Dutchman's, and ye was balancin' on the plank at this minit."

"Come and see for yourself," answered Wild Bill, "and give me a lift. Once in your cabin, and in front of your fire, I'll answer all the questions you may ask. But I'll answer no more until I'm inside the door."

"Ye be sartinly sober to-night," answered the Trapper, laughing, as he started down the hill, "fur ye talk sense, and that's more'n a man can do when he talks through the nozzle of a bottle."

"Lord-a-massy!" exclaimed the old man as he stood over the sled, and saw the huge box that was on it. "Lord-a-massy, Bill! what a tug ye must have had! and how ye come to be sober with sech a load behind ye is beyond the reckinin' of a man who has knowed ye nigh on to twenty year. I never knowed ye disapp'int one arter this fashion afore."

"It is strange, I confess," answered Wild Bill, appreciating the humor that lurked in the honesty of the old man's utterance. "It is strange, that's a fact, for it's Christmas Eve, and I ought to be roaring drunk at the Dutchman's this very minit, according to custom; but I pledged him to get the box through jest as he wanted it done, and that I wouldn't touch a drop of liquor until I had done it. And here it is according to promise, for here I am sober, and here is his box."

"H'ist along, Bill, h'ist along!" exclaimed the Trapper, who suddenly became alive with interest, for he surmised whence the box had come. "H'ist along, Bill, I say, and have done with yer talkin', and let's see what ye have got on yer sled. It's strange that a man of your sense will stand jibberin' here in the snow with a roarin' fire within a dozen rods of ye."

Whatever retort Wild Bill may have contemplated, it was effectually prevented by the energy with which the Trapper pushed the sled after him. Indeed, it was all he could do to keep it off his heels, so earnestly did the old man propel it from behind; and so, with many a slip and scramble on the part of Wild Bill, and a continued muttering on the part of the Trapper about the "nonsense of a man's jibberin' in the snow arter a twenty-mile drag, with a good fire within a dozen rods of him," the sled was shot through the doorway into the cabin, and stood fully revealed in the bright blaze of the firelight.

"Take off yer coat and yer moccasins, Wild Bill," exclaimed the Trapper, as he closed the door, "and git in front of the fire; pull out the coals, and set the tea-pot a-steepin'. The yarb will take the chill out of ye better than the pizen of the Dutchman. Ye'll find a haunch of venison in the cupboard that I roasted to-day, and some johnny-cake; I doubt ef either be cold. Help yerself, help yerself, Bill, while I take a peep at the box."

No one can appreciate the intensity of the old man's feelings in reference to the mysterious box, unless he calls to mind the strictness with which he was wont to interpret and fulfil the duties of hospitality. To him the coming of a guest was a welcome event, and the service which the latter might require of the host both a sacred and pleasant obligation. To serve a guest with his own hand, which he did with a natural courtesy peculiar to himself, was his delight. Nor did it matter with him what the quality of the guest might be. The wandering trapper or the vagabond Indian was served with as sincere attention as the richest visitor from the city. But now his feelings were so stirred by the sight of the box thus strangely brought to him, and by his surmise touching who the sender might be, that Wild Bill was left to help himself without the old man's attendance.

It was evident that Bill was equal to the occasion, and was not aware of the slightest neglect. At least, his actions were not, by the neglect of the Trapper, rendered less decided, or the quality of his appetite affected, for the examination he made of the old man's cupboard, and the familiarity with which he handled the contents, made it evident that he was not in the least abashed, or uncertain how to proceed; for he attacked the provisions with the energy of a man who had fasted long, and who has at last not only come suddenly to an ample supply of food, but also feels that for a few moments, at least, he will be unobserved. The Trapper turned toward the box, and approached it for a deliberate examination.

"The boards be sawed," he said, "and they come from the mills of the settlement, for the smoothin'-plane has been over 'em." Then he inspected the jointing, and noted how truly the edges were drawn.

"The box has come a goodly distance," he said to himself, "fur there isn't a workman this side of the Horicon that could j'int it in that fashion. There sartinly orter be some letterin', or a leetle bit of writin', somewhere about the chest, tellin' who the box belonged to, and to whom it was sent." Saying this, the old man unlashed the box from the sled, and rolled it over, so that the side might come uppermost. As no direction appeared on the smoothly planed surface, he rolled it half over again. A little white card neatly tacked to the board was now revealed. The Trapper stooped, and on the card read,—

JOHN NORTON,
TO THE CARE OF WILD BILL.

"Yis, the 'J' be his'n," muttered the old man, as he spelled out the word J-o-h-n, "and the big 'N' be as plain as an otter-trail in the snow. The boy don't make his letters overplain, as I conceit, but the 'J' and the 'N' be his'n." And then he paused for a full minute, his head bowed over the box. "The boy don't forget," he murmured, and he wiped his eyes with the back of his hand. "The boy don't forget." And then he added, "No, he isn't one of the forgittin' kind. Wild Bill," said the Trapper, as he turned toward that personage, whose attack on the venison haunch was as determined as ever, "Wild Bill, this box be from Henry!"

"I shouldn't wonder," answered that individual, speaking from a mass of edibles that filled his mouth.

"And it be a Christmas gift!" continued the old man.

"It looks so," returned Bill, as laconically as before.

"And it be a mighty heavy box!" said the Trapper.

"You'd 'a' thought so, if you had dragged it over the mile-and-a-half carry. It was good sleddin' on the river, but the carry took the stuff out of me."

"Very like, very like," responded the Trapper; "fur the gullies be deep on the carry, and it must have been slippery haulin'. Didn't ye git a leetle 'arnest in yer feelin's, Bill, afore ye got to the top of the last ridge?"

"Old man," answered Bill as he wheeled his chair toward the Trapper, with a pint cup of tea in the one hand, and wiping his mustache with the coat-sleeve of the other, "I got it to the top three times, or within a dozen feet from the top, and each time it got away from me and went to the bottom agin; for the roots was slippery, and I couldn't git a grip on the toe of my moccasins; but I held on the rope, and I got to the bottom neck and neck with the sled every time."

"Ye did well, ye did well," responded the Trapper, laughing; "fur a loaded sled goes down hill mighty fast when the slide is a steep un, and a man who gits to the bottom as quick as the sled must have a good grip, and be considerably in 'arnest. But ye got her up finally by the same path, didn't ye?"

"Yes, I got her up," returned Bill. "The fourth time I went for that ridge, I fetched her to the top, for I was madder than a hornet."

"And what did ye do, Bill?" continued the Trapper. "What did ye do when ye got to the top?"

"I jest tied that sled to a sapling so it wouldn't git away agin, and I got on to the top of that box, and I talked to that gulch a minit or two in a way that satisfied my feelings."

"I shouldn't wonder," answered the Trapper, laughing, "fur ye must have been a good deal riled. But ye did well to git the box through, and ye got here in time, and ye've 'arnt yer wages; and now, ef ye'll tell me how much I am to pay ye, ye shall have yer money, and ye needn't scrimp yourself on the price, Wild Bill, for the drag has been a hard un; so tell me yer price, and I'll count ye out the money."

"Old man," answered Bill, "I didn't bring that box through for money, and I won't take a"—

Perhaps Wild Bill was about to emphasize his refusal by some verbal addition to the simple statement, but, if it was his intention, he checked himself, and said, "a cent."

"It's well said," answered the Trapper; "yis, it's well said, and does jestice to yer feelin's, I don't doubt; but an extra pair of breeches one of these days wouldn't hurt ye, and the money won't come amiss."

"I tell ye, old man," returned Wild Bill earnestly, "I won't take a cent. I'll allow there's several colors in my trousers, for I've patched in a dozen different pieces off and on, and I doubt, as ye hint, if the patching holds together much longer; but I've eaten at your table and slept in your cabin more than once, John Norton, and whether I've come to it sober or drunk, your door was never shut in my face, and I don't forget either that the man who sent you that box fished me from the creek one day, when I had walked into it with two bottles of the Dutchman's whiskey in my pocket, and not one cent of your money or his will I take for bringing the box in to you."

"Have it yer own way, ef ye will," said the Trapper; "but I won't forget the deed ye have did, and the boy won't forget it neither. Come, let's clear away the vict'als, and we'll open the box. It's sartinly a big un, and I would like to see what he has put inside of it."

The opening of the box was a spectacle such as gladdens the heart to see. At such moments the countenance of the Trapper was as facile in the changefulness of its expression as that of a child. The passing feelings of his soul found an adequate mirror in his face, as the white clouds of a summer day find full reflection in the depth of a tranquil lake. He was not too old or too learned to be wise, for the wisdom of hearty happiness was his,—the wisdom of being glad, and gladly showing it.

As for Wild Bill, the best of his nature was in the ascendant, and with the curiosity and pleasure of a child, and a happiness as sincere as if the box was his own, he assisted at the opening.

"The man who made this box did the work in a workmanlike fashion," said the Trapper, as he strove to insert the edge of his hatchet into the jointing of the cover, "fur he shet these boards together like the teeth of a bear-trap when the bars be well 'iled. It's a pity the boy didn't send him along with the box, Wild Bill, fur it sartinly looks as ef we should have to kindle a fire on it, and burn a hole in through the cover."

At last, by dint of great exertion, and with the assistance of Wild Bill and the poker, the cover of the box was wrenched off, and the contents were partially revealed.

"Glory to God, Wild Bill!" exclaimed the Trapper. "Here be yer breeches!" and he held up a pair of pantaloons made of the stoutest Scotch stuff. "Yis, here be yer breeches, fur here on the waistband be pinned a bit of paper, and on it be written, 'Fur Wild Bill.' And here be a vest to match; and here be a jacket; and here be two pairs of socks in the pockets of the jacket; and here be two woollen shirts, one packed away in each sleeve. And here!" shouted the old man, as he turned up the lapel of the coat, "Wild Bill, look here! Here be a five-dollar note!" and the old man swung one of the socks over his head, and shouted, "Hurrah for Wild Bill!" And the two hounds, catching the enthusiasm of their master, lifted their muzzles into the air, and bayed deep and long, till the cabin fairly shook with the joyful uproar of man and dogs.

It is doubtful if any gift ever took the recipient more by surprise than this bestowed upon Wild Bill. It is true that, judged by the law of strict deserts, the poor fellow had not deserved much of the world, and certainly the world had not forgotten to be strictly just in his case, for it had not given him much. It is a question if he had ever received a gift before in all his life, certainly not one of any considerable value. His reception of this generous and thoughtful provision for his wants was characteristic both of his training and his nature.

The old Trapper, as he had ended his cheering, flung the pantaloons, the vest, the jacket, the socks, the shirts, and the money into his lap.

For a moment the poor fellow sat looking at the warm and costly garments that he held in his hands, silent in an astonishment too profound for speech, and then, recovering the use of his organs, he gasped forth,—

"I swear!" and then broke down, and sobbed like a child.

The Trapper, kneeling beside the box, looked at the poor fellow with a face radiant with happiness, while his mouth was stretched with laughter, utterly unconsious that tears were brimming his own eyes.

"Old Trapper," said Wild Bill, rising to his feet, and holding the garments forth in his hands, "this is the first present I ever received in my life. I have been kicked and cussed, sneered at and taunted, and I deserved it all. But no man ever gave me a lift, or showed he cared a cent whether I starved or froze, lived or died. You know, John Norton, what a fool I've been, and what has ruined me, and that when sober I'm more of a man than many who hoot me. And here I swear, old man, that while a button is on this jacket, or two threads of these breeches hold together, I'll never touch a drop of liquor, sick or well, living or dying, so help me God! and there's my hand on it."

"Amen!" exclaimed the Trapper, as he sprang to his feet, and clasped in his own strong palm the hand that the other had stretched out to him. "The Lord in his marcy be nigh ye when tempted, Bill, and keep ye true to yer pledge!"

Of all the pleasant sights that the angels of God, looking from their high homes, saw on earth that Christmas Eve, perhaps not one was dearer in their eyes than the spectacle here described,— the two sturdy men standing with their bands clasped in solemn pledge of the reformation of the one, and the helping sympathy of the other, above that Christmas-box in the cabin in the woods.

It is not necessary to follow in detail the Trapper's further examination of the box. The reader's imagination, assisted by many a happy reminiscence, will enable him to realize the scene. There was a small keg of powder, a large plug of lead, a little chest of tea, a bag of sugar, and also one of coffee. There were nails, matches, thread, buttons, a woollen under-jacket, a pair of mittens, and a cap of choicest fur, made of an otter's skin that Henry himself had trapped a year before. All these and other packages were taken out one by one, carefully examined, and characteristically commented on by the Trapper, and passed to Wild Bill, who in turn inspected and commented on them, and then laid them carefully on the table. Beneath these packages was a thin board, constituting a sort of division between its upper and lower half.

"There seems to be a sort of cellar to this box," said the Trapper, as he sat looking at the division. "I shouldn't be surprised ef the boy himself was in here somewhere, so be ready, Bill, fur anything, fur the Lord only knows what's underneath this board." Saying which, the old man thrust his hand under one end of the division, and pulled out a bundle loosely tied with a string, which became unfastened as the Trapper lifted the roll from its place in the box, and, as he shook it open, and held its contents at arm's length up to the light, the startled eyes of Wild Bill, and the earnest gaze of the Trapper, beheld a woman's dress!

"Heavens and 'arth, Bill!" exclaimed the Trapper, "what's this?" And then a flash of light crossed his face, in the illumination of which the look of wonder vanished, and, dropping upon his knees, he flung the dividing board out of the box, and his companion and himself saw at a glance what was underneath.

Children's shoes, and dresses of warmest stuffs; tippets and mittens; a full suit for a little boy, boots and all; a jack-knife and whistle; two dolls dressed in brave finery, with flaxen hair and blue eyes; a little hatchet; a huge ball of yarn, and a hundred and one things needed in the household; and underneath all a Bible; and under that a silver star on a blue field, and pinned to the silk a scrap of paper, on which was written,—

"Hang this over the picture of the lad."

"Ay, ay," said the Trapper in a tremulous voice, as he looked at the silver star, "it shall be done as ye say, boy; but the lad has got beyond the clouds, and is walkin' a trail that is lighted from eend to eend by a light clearer and brighter than ever come from the shinin' of any star. I hope we may be found worthy to walk it with him, boy, when we, too, have come to the edge of the Great Clearin'."

To the Trapper it was perfectly evident for whom the contents of the box were intended; but the sender had left nothing in doubt, for, when the old man had lifted from the floor the board that he had flung out, he discovered some writing traced with heavy pencilling on the wood, and which without much effort he spelled out to Wild Bill,—

"Give these on Christmas Day to the woman at the dismal hut, and a merry Christmas to you all."

"Ay, ay," said the Trapper, "it shall be did, barrin' accident, as ye say; and a merry Christmas it'll make fur us all. Lord-a-massy! what *will* the poor woman say when she and her leetle uns git these warm garments on? There be no trouble about fillin' the basket now; no, I sartinly can't git half of the stuff in. Wild Bill, I guess ye'll have to do some more sleddin' to-morrow, fur these presents must go over the mountain in the mornin', ef we have to harness up the pups." And then he told his companion of the poor woman and the children, and his intended visit to them on the morrow.

"I fear," he said, "that they be havin' a hard time of it, 'specially ef her husband has desarted her."

"Little good would he do her, if he was with her," answered Wild Bill, "for he's a lazy knave when he's sober, and a thief as well, as you and I know, John Norton; for he's fingered our traps more than once, and swapped the skins for liquor at the Dutchman's; but he's thieved once too many times, for the folks in the settlement has ketched him in the act, and they put him in the jail for six months, as I heard day before yesterday."

"I'm glad on't; yis, I'm glad on't," answered the Trapper; "and I hope they'll keep him there till they've larnt him how to work. I've had my eye on the knave fur a good while, and the last time I seed him I told him ef he fingered any more of my traps, I'd larn him the commandments in a way he wouldn't forgit; and, as I had him in hand, and felt a leetle like talkin' that mornin', I gin him a piece of my mind, techin' his treatment of his wife and leetle uns, that he didn't relish, I fancy, fur he winced and squirmed like a fox in a trap. Yis, I'm glad they've got the knave, and I hope they'll keep him till he's answered fur his misdoin'; but I'm sartinly afeered the poor woman be havin' a hard time of it."

"I fear so, too," answered Wild Bill; "and if I can do anything to help you in your plans, jest say the word, and I'm your man to back or haul, jest as you want me."

And so it was arranged that they should go over the mountain together on the morrow, and take the provisions and the gifts that were in the box to the poor woman; and, after talking awhile of the happiness their visit would give, the two men, happy in their thoughts, and with their hearts full of that peace which passeth the understanding of the selfish, laid themselves down to sleep;

and over the two,— the one. drawing to the close of an honorable and well-spent life, the other standing at the middle of a hitherto useless existence, but facing the future with a noble resolution,— over the two, as they slept, the angels of Christmas kept their watch.

II.

On the other side of the mountain stood the dismal hut; and the stars of that blessed eve had shone down upon the lonely clearing in which it stood, and the smooth white surface of the frozen and snow-covered lake which lay in front of it, as brightly as they had shone on the cabin of the Trapper; but no friendly step had made its trail in the surrounding snow, and no blessed gift had been brought to its solitary door.

As the evening wore on, the great clearing round about it remained drearily void of sound or motion, and filled only with the white stillness of the frosty, snow-lighted night. Once, indeed, a wolf stole from underneath the dark balsams into the white silence, and, running up a huge log that lay aslant a ledge of rocks, looked across and round the great opening in the woods, stood a moment, then gave a shivering sort of a yelp, and scuttled back under the shadows of the forest, as if its darkness was warmer than the frozen stillness of the open space. An owl, perched somewhere amid the pine-tops, snug and warm within the cover of its arctic plumage, engaged from time to time in solemn gossip with some neighbor that lived on the opposite shore of the lake. And once a raven, roosting on the dry bough of a lightning-blasted pine, dreamed that the white moonlight was the light of dawn, and began to stir his sable wings, and croak a harsh welcome; but awakened by his blunder, and ashamed of his mistake, he broke off in the very midst of his discordant call, and again settled gloomily down amid his black plumes to his interrupted repose, making by his sudden silence the surrounding silence more silent than before. It seemed as if the very angels, who, we are taught, fly abroad over all the earth that blessed night, carrying gifts to every household, had forgotten the cabin in the woods, and had left it to the cold hospitality of unsympathetic nature.

Within the lonely hut, which thus seemed forgotten of Heaven itself, sat a woman huddling her young—two girls and a boy. The fireplace was of monstrous proportions, and the chimney yawned upward so widely that one looking up the sooty passage might see the stars shining overhead. A little fire burned feebly in the huge stone recess: scant warmth might such a fire yield, kindled in such a fireplace, to those around it. Indeed, the little flame seemed conscious of its own inability, and burned with a wavering and mistrustful flicker, as if it was discouraged in view of the task set before it, and had more than half concluded to go out altogether.

The cabin was of large size, and undivided into apartments. The little fire was only able to illuminate the central section, and more than half of the room was hidden in utter darkness. The woman's face, which the faint flame over which she was crouched revealed with painful clearness, showed pale and haggard. The induration of exposure and the tightening lines of hunger sharpened and marred a countenance which, a happier fortune would have kept even comely. It had that old look about it which comes from wretchedness rather than age, and the weariness of its expression was pitiful to see. Was it work or vain waiting for happier fortunes that made her look so tired? Alas! the weariness of waiting for what we long for, and long for purely, but which never comes! Is it the work or the longing—the long longing—that has put the silver in your head, friend, and scarred the smooth bloom of your cheeks, my lady, with those ugly lines?

"Mother, I'm hungry," said the little boy, looking up into the woman's face. "Can't I have just a little more to eat?"

"Be still," answered the woman sharply, speaking in the tones of vexed inability. "I've given you almost the last morsel in the house."

The boy said nothing more, but nestled up more closely to his mother's knee, and stuck one little stockingless foot out until the cold toes were half hidden in the ashes. O warmth! blessed warmth! how pleasant art thou to old and young alike! Thou art the emblem of life, as thy absence is the evidence and sign of life's cold opposite. Would that all the cold toes in the world could get to my grate to-night, and all the shivering ones be gathered

to this fireside! Ay, and that the children of poverty, that lack for
bread, might get their hungry hands into that well-filled cupboard
there, too!

In a moment the woman said, "You children had better go to bed. You'll be warmer in the rags than in this miserable fireplace."

The words were harshly spoken, as if the very presence of the children, cold and hungry as they were, was a vexation to her; and they moved off in obedience to her command.

O cursed poverty! I know thee to be of Satan, for I myself have eaten at thy scant table, and slept in thy cold bed. And never yet have I seen thee bring one smile to human lips, or dry one tear as it fell from a human eye. But I have seen thee sharpen the tongue for biting speech, and harden the tender heart. Ay, I've seen thee make even the presence of love a burden, and cause the mother to wish that the puny babe nursing her scant breast had never been born. And so the children went to their unsightly bed, and silence reigned in the hut.

"Mother," said one of the girls, speaking out of the darkness,—"mother, isn't this Christmas Eve?"

"Yes," answered the woman sharply. "Go to sleep." And again there was silence.

Happy is childhood, that amid whatever deprivation and misery it can so weary itself in the day that when night comes on it can lose in the forgetfulness of slumber its sorrows and wants!

Thus, while the children lost the sense of their unhappy surroundings, including the keen pangs of hunger, for a time, and under the tattered blankets that covered them saw, perhaps, visions of enchanting lands, and in their dreams feasted at those wonderful tables which hungry children see only in sleep, to the poor woman sitting at the failing fire there came no surcease of sorrow, and no vision threw even an evanescent brightness over the hard, cold facts of her surroundings. And the reality of her condition was dire enough, God knows. Alone in the wilderness, miles from any human habitation, the trails covered deep with snow, her provisions exhausted, actual suffering already upon them, and starvation staring them squarely in the face. No wonder that her soul sank within her; no wonder that her thoughts turned toward bitterness.

"Yes, it's Christmas Eve," she muttered, "and the rich will keep it gayly. God sends them presents enough; but you see if he remembers me! Oh, they may talk about the angels of Christmas Eve flying abroad to-night, loaded with gifts, but they'll fly mighty

high above this shanty, I reckon; no, they won't even drop a piece
of meat as they soar past." And so she sat muttering and moaning
over her woes, and they were heavy enough,—too heavy for her
poor soul, unassisted, to lift,—while the flame on the hearth grew
thinner and thinner, until it had no more warmth in it than the
shadow of a ghost, and, like its resemblance, was about to flit and
fade away. At last she said, in a softened tone, as if the remembrance of the Christmas legend had softened her surly thoughts
and sweetened the bitter mood,—

"Perhaps I'm wrong to take on so. Perhaps it isn't God's fault
that I and my children are deserted and starving. But why should
the innocent be punished for the guilty, and why should the
wicked have enough and to spare, while those who do no evil go
half naked and starved?"

Alas, poor woman! that puzzle has puzzled many besides thee,
and many lips besides thine have asked that question, querulously
or entreatingly, many a time; but whether they asked it in vexation
and rebellion of spirit, or humbly besought Heaven to answer, to
neither murmur nor prayer did Heaven vouchsafe a response. Is
it because we are so small, or, being small, are so inquisitive, that
the Great Oracle of the blue remains so dumb when we cry?

At this point the poor little flame, as if unable to abide the
cold much longer, flared fitfully, and uneasily shifted itself from
brand to brand, threatening with many a flicker to go out; but the
woman, with her elbows on her knees, and her face settled firmly
between her hands, still sat with eyes that saw not the feeble flame
at which they so steadily gazed.

"I will do it, *I will do it!*" she suddenly exclaimed. "I will make
one more effort. They shall not starve while I have strength to
try. Perhaps God will aid me. They say he always does at the last
pinch, and he certainly sees that I am there now. I wonder if he's
been waiting for me to get just where I am before he helped me?
There is one more chance left, and I'll make the trial. I'll go down
to the shore where I saw the big tracks in the snow. It's a long
way, but I shall get there somehow. If God is going to be good
to me, he won't let me freeze or faint on the way. Yes, I'll creep
into bed now, and try and get a little sleep, for I must be strong in
the morning." And with these words the poor woman crept off to
her bed, and burrowed down, more like an animal than a human

being, beside her little ones, as they lay huddled close together and asleep, down in the rags.

What angel was it that followed her to her miserable couch, and stirred kindly feelings in her bosom? Some sweet one, surely; for she shortly lifted herself to a sitting posture, and, gently drawing down the old blanket with which the children, for warmth's sake, had wrapped their heads, looked as only a mother might at the three little faces lying side by side, and, bending tenderly over them, she placed a gentle kiss upon the forehead of each; then she nestled down again in her own place, and said, "Perhaps God will help me." And with this sentence, half a prayer and half a doubt, born on the one hand from that sweet faith which never quite deserts a woman's bosom, and on the other from that bitter experience which had made her seem in her own eyes deserted of God, she fell asleep.

She, too, dreamed; but her dreaming was only the prolongation of her waking thoughts; for long after her eyes closed she moved uneasily on her hard couch, and muttered, "Perhaps God will. Perhaps"—

Sad is it for us who are old enough to have tasted the bitterness of that cup which life sooner or later presents to all lips, and have borne the burden of its toil and fretting, that our vexations and disappointments pursue us even in our slumber, disturbing our sleep with reproachful visions and the sound of voices whose upbraiding robs us of our otherwise peaceful repose. Perhaps somewhere in the years to come, after much wandering and weariness, guided of God, we may come to that fountain of which the ancients dreamed, and for which the noblest among them sought so long, and died seeking; plunging into which, we shall find our lost youth in its cool depths, and, rising refreshed and strengthened, shall go on our eternal journey re-clothed with the beauty, the innocence, and the happiness of our youth.

The poor woman slept uneasily, and with much muttering to herself; but the rapid hours slid noiselessly down the icy grooves of night, and soon the cold morning put its white face against the frozen windows of the east, and peered shiveringly forth. Who says the earth cannot look as cold and forbidding as the human countenance ? The sky hung over the frozen world like a dome of gray steel, whose invisibly matched plates were riveted here and there by a few white, gleaming stars. The surface of the snow sparkled with crystals that flashed colorlessly cold. The air seemed armed, and full of sharp, eager points that pricked the skin painfully. The great tree-trunks cracked their sharp protests against the frosty entrances being made beneath their bark. The lake, from under the smothering ice, roared in dismay and pain, and sent the thunders of its wrath at its imprisonment around the resounding shores. A bitter morn, a bitter morn,—ah me! a bitter morn for the poor!

The woman, wakened by the gray light, moved in the depths of the tattered blankets, sat upright, rubbed her eyes with her hands, looked about her as if to recall her scattered senses, and then, as thought returned, crept stealthily out of the hole in which she had lain, that she might not wake the children, who, coiled together, slumbered on, still closely clasped in the arms of blessed unconsciousness.

"They had better sleep," she said to herself. "If I fail to bring them meat, I hope they will never wake!"

Ah! if the poor woman could only have foreseen the bitter disappointment, or that other something which the future was to bring her, would she have made that prayer? Is it best for us, as some say, that we cannot see what is coming, but must weep on till the last tear is shed, uncheered by the sweet fortune so nigh, or laugh unchecked until the happy tones are mingled with, and smothered by, the rising moan? Is it best, I wonder?

She noiselessly gathered together what additions she could make to her garments, and then, taking down the rifle from its hangings, opened the door, and stepped forth into the outer cold. There was a look of brave determination in her eyes as she faced the chilly greeting the world gave her, and with more of hopefulness than had before appeared upon her countenance, she struck bravely off along the lake shore, which at this point receded toward the mountain.

For an hour she kept steadily on, with her eyes constantly on the alert for the least sign of the wished and prayed-for game. Suddenly she stopped, and crouched down in the snow, peering straight ahead. Well might she seek concealment, for there, standing on a point of land that jutted sharply out into the lake, not forty rods away, unscreened and plain to view, stood a buck of such goodly proportions as one even in years of hunting might not see.

The woman's eyes fairly gleamed as she saw the noble animal standing thus in full sight; but who may tell the agony of fear and hope that filled her bosom! The buck stood lordly erect, facing the east, as if he would do homage to, or receive homage from, the rising sun, whose yellow beams fell full upon his uplifted front. The thought of her mind, the fear of her heart, were plain. The buck would soon move; when he moved, which way would he move? Would he go from or come toward her? Would she get him, or would she lose him? Oh, the agony of that thought!

"God of the starving," burst from her quivering lips, "let not my children die!"

Many prayers more ornate rose that day to Him whose ears are open to all cries. But of all that prayed on that Christmas morn, whether with few words or many, surely, no heart rose with the seeking words more earnestly than the poor woman kneeling as she prayed, rifle in hand, amid the snow.

"God of the starving, let not my children die!"

That was her prayer; and, as if in answer to her agonizing petition, the buck turned and began to advance directly toward her, browsing as he came. Once he stopped, looked around, and snuffed the air suspiciously. Had he scented her presence, and would he bound away? Should she fire now? No; her judgment told her she could not trust the gun or her aim at such a range. He must come nigher,—come even to the big maple, and stand there, not ten rods away; then she felt sure she should get him. So she waited. Oh, how the cold ate into her! How her teeth chattered as the chills ran their torturing courses through her thin, shivering frame! But still she clutched the cold barrel, and still she watched and waited, and still she prayed,—

"God of the starving, let not my children die!"

Alas, poor woman! My own body shivers as I think of thine, and my pen falters to write what misery befell thee on that wretched morn.

Did the buck turn? Did he, having come so tantalizingly near, retrace his steps? No. He continued to advance. Had Heaven heard her prayer? Her soul answered it had; and with such feelings in it toward Him to whom she had appealed as she had not felt in all her life before, she steadied herself for the. shot. For even as she prayed, the deer came on,—came to the big maple, and lifted his muzzle to its highest reach to seize with his tongue a thin streamer of moss that lay against the smooth bark. There he stood, his blue-brown side full toward her, unconscious of her presence. Noiselessly she cocked the piece. Noiselessly she raised it to her face, and with every nerve drawn to its tightest tension, sighted the noble game, and—*fired*.

Had the frosty air watered her eye? was it a tear of joy and gratitude that dimmed the clearness of its sight? or were the half-frozen fingers unable to steady the cold barrel at the instant of its

explosion? We know not. We only know that in spite of prayer, in spite of noblest effort, she missed the game. For, as the rifle cracked, the buck gave a snort of fear, and with swift bounds flew up the mountain; while the poor woman, dropping the gun with a groan, fell fainting on the snow.

III.

At the same moment the rifle sounded, two men, the Trapper with his pack, and Wild Bill with his sled heavily loaded, were descending the western slope of the mountain, not a mile from the clearing in which stood the lonely cabin. The sound of the piece brought them to a halt as quickly as if the bullet had cut through the air in front of their faces. For several minutes both stood in the attitude of listening.

"Down into the snow with ye, pups!" exclaimed the Trapper, in a hoarse whisper. "Down into the snow with ye, I say! Rover, ef ye lift yer muzzle agin, l'll warm yer back with the ramrod. By the Lord, Bill, the buck is comin' this way; ye can see his horns lift above the leetle balsams as he breaks through the thicket yender. Ef he strikes the runway, he'll sartinly come within range;" and the old Trapper slipped his arms from the pack, and, lowering it to the earth, sank on his knees beside it, where he waited as motionless as if the breath had departed his body.

Onward came the game. As the Trapper had suggested, the buck, with mighty and far-reaching bounds, cleared the shrubby obstructions, and, entering the runway, tore up the familiar path with the violence of a tornado. Onward he came, his head flung upward, his antlers laid well back, tongue lolling from his mouth, and his nostrils smoking with the hot breaths that burst in streaming columns from them. Not until his swift career had brought him exactly in front of his position did the old man stir a muscle. But then, quick as the motion of the leaping game, his rifle jumped to his cheek, and even as the buck was at the central point of his leap, and suspended in the air, the piece cracked sharp and clear, and the deer, stricken to his death, fell with a crash to the ground. The quivering hounds rose to their feet, and bayed long

and deep; Wild Bill swung his hat and yelled; and for a moment the woods rang with the wild cries of dogs and man.

"Lord-a-massy, Bill, what a mouth ye have when ye open it!" exclaimed the Trapper, as he leisurely poured the powder into the still smoking barrel. "Atween ye and the pups, it's enough to drive a man crazy. I should sartinly think ye had never seed a deer shot afore, by the way ye be actin'."

"I've seen a good many, as you know, John Norton; but I never saw one tumbled over by a single bullet when at the very top of his jump, as that one was. I surely thought you had waited too long, and I wouldn't have given a cent for your chances when you pulled. It was a wonderful shot, John Norton, and I would take just such another tramp as I have had, to see you do it again, old man."

"It wasn't bad," returned the Trapper; "no, it sartinly wasn't bad, fur he was goin' as ef the Old Harry was arter him. I shouldn't wonder ef he had felt the tech of lead down there in the holler, and the smart of his hurt kept him fly in'. Let's go and look him over, and see ef we can't find the markin's of the bullit on him."

In a moment the two stood above the dead deer.

"It is as I thought," said the Trapper, as he pointed with his ram-rod to a stain of blood on one of the hams of the buck. "The bullit drove through his thigh here, but it didn't tech the bone, and was a sheer waste of lead, fur it only sot him goin' like an arrer. Bill, I sartinly doubt," continued the old man, as he measured the noble animal with his eye, "I sartinly doubt ef I ever seed a bigger deer. There's seven prongs on his horns, and I'd bet a horn of powder agin a chargerful that he'd weigh three hundred pounds as he lies. Lord, what a Christmas gift he'll be fur the woman! The skin will make a blanket fit fur a queen to sleep under, and the meat, jedi-ciously cared for, will last her all winter. We must manage to git it to the edge of the clearin', anyhow, or the wolves might make free with our venison, Bill. Yer sled is a strong un, and it'll bear the loadin', ef ye go keerful."

The Trapper and his companion set themselves to their task with the energy of men accustomed to surmount every obstacle, and in a short half-hour the sled, with its double loading, stopped at the door of the lonely cabin.

"I don't understand this, Wild Bill," said the Trapper. "Here be a woman's tracks in the snow, and the door be left a leetle ajar, but there be no smoke in the chimney, and they sartinly ain't very noisy inside. I'll jest give a knock or two, and see ef they be stirrin';" and, suiting the action to the word, he knocked long and loud on the large door. But to his noisy summons there came no response, and without a moment of farther hesitation he shoved open the door, and entered.

"God of marcy! Wild Bill," exclaimed the Trapper, "look in here!"

A huge room dimly lighted, holes in the roof, here and there a heap of snow on the floor, an immense fireplace with no fire in it, and a group of scared, wild-looking children huddled together in the farther corner, like young and timid animals that had fled in affright from the nest where they had slept, at some fearful intrusion. That is what the Trapper saw.

"I"—Whatever Wild Bill was about to say, his astonishment, and we may add his pity, were too profound for him to complete his ejaculation.

"Don't ye be afeerd, leetle uns," said the Trapper, as he advanced into the centre of the room to more fully survey the wretched place. "This be Christmas morn, and me and Wild Bill and the pups have come over the mountain to wish ye all a merry Christmas. But where be yer mother?" queried the old man, as he looked kindly at the startled group.

"We don't know where she is," answered the older of the two girls; "we thought she was in bed with us, till you woke us. We don't know where she has gone."

"I have it, I have it, Wild Bill!" exclaimed the Trapper, whose eyes had been busy scanning the place while talking with the children. "The rifle be gone from the hangings, and the tracks in the snow be hern. Yis, yis, 1 see it all. She went out in hope of gittin' the leetle uns here somethin' to eat, and that was her rifle we heerd, and her bullet made that hole in the ham of the buck. What a disapp'intment to the poor creetur when she seed she hadn't hit him! Her heart eena'most broke, I dare say. But the Lord was in it—leastwise, he didn't go ag'in the proper shapin' of things arterwards. Come, Bill, let's stir round lively, and get the shanty in shape a leetle, and some vict'als on the table afore she comes. Yis, git out yer axe, and slash into that dead beech at the corner of the cabin, while I sorter clean up inside. A fire is the fust thing on sech a mornin' as this; so scurry round, Bill, and bring in the wood as ef ye was a good deal in 'arnest, and do ye cut to the measure of the fireplace, and don't waste yer time in shortenin' it, fur the longer the fireplace, the longer the wood; that is, ef ye want to make it a heater."

His companion obeyed with alacrity; and by the time the Trapper had cleaned out the snow, and swept down the soot from the sides of the fireplace, and put things partially to rights, Bill had stacked the dry logs into the huge opening, nearly to the upper jamb, and, with the help of some large sheets of birch-bark, kindled them to a flame. "Come here, leetle uns," said the Trapper, as he turned his good-natured face toward the children,—"come here, and put yer leetle feet on the h'arthstun, fur it's warmin', and I conceit yer toes be about freezin'."

It was not in the power of children to withstand the attraction of such an invitation, extended with such a hearty voice and such benevolence of feature. The children came promptly forward, and stood in a row on the great stone, and warmed their little shivering bodies by the abundant flames.

"Now, leetle folks," said the Trapper, "jest git yerselves well warmed, then git on what clothes ye've got, and we'll have some breakfast,—yis, we'll have breakfast ready by the time yer mother gits back, fur I know where she be gone, and she'll be hungry and cold when she gits in. I don't conceit that this little chap here can help much, but ye girls be big enough to help a good deal. So, when ye be warm, do ye put away the bed to the furderest corner, and shove out the table in front of the fire, and put on the dishes, sech as ye have, and be smart about it, too, fur yer mother will sartinly be comin' soon, and we must be ahead of her with the cookin'."

What a change the next half-hour made in the appearance of the cabin! The huge fire sent its heat to the farthest corner of the great room. The miserable bed had been removed out of sight, and the table, drawn up in front of the fire, was set with the needed dishes. On the hearthstone a large platter of venison steak, broiled by the Trapper's skill, simmered in the heat. A mighty pile of cakes, brown to a turn, flanked one side, while a stack of potatoes baked in the ashes supported the other. The teapot sent forth its refreshing odor through the room. The children, with their faces washed and hair partially, at least, combed, ran about with bare feet on the warm floor, comfortable and happy. To them it was as a beautiful dream. The breakfast was ready, and the visitors sat waiting for the coming of her to whose assistance the angel of Christmas Eve had sent them.

"Sh!" whispered the Trapper, whose quick ear had caught the sound of a dragging step in the snow. "She's comin'!"

Too weary and faint, too sick at heart and exhausted in body to observe the unaccustomed signs of human presence around her dwelling, the poor woman dragged herself to the door, and opened it. The gun she still held in her hand fell rattling to the floor, and, with eyes wildly opened, she gazed bewildered at the spectacle. The blazing fire, the set table, the food on the hearthstone, the smiling children, the two men! She passed her hands across her eyes as one waking from sleep. Was she dreaming? Was this cabin the miserable hut she had left at daybreak? Was that the same fireplace in front of whose cold and cheerless recess she had crouched the night before? And were those two strangers there men, or were they angels? Was what she saw real, or was it only a fevered vision born of her weakness?

Her senses actually reeled to and fro, and she trembled for a moment on the verge of unconsciousness. Indeed, the shock was so overwhelming that in another instant she would have swooned and fallen to the floor had not the growing faintness been checked by the sound of a human voice.

"A merry Christmas to ye, my good woman," said the Trapper. "A merry Christmas to ye and yourn!"

The woman started as the hearty tones fell on her ear, and, steadying herself by the door, she said, speaking as one partially dazed,—

"Are you John Norton the Trapper, or are you an ang—"

"Ye needn't sight agin," interrupted the old man. "Yis, I'm old John Norton himself, nothin' better and nothin' wuss; and the man in the chair here by my side is Wild Bill, and ye couldn't make an angel out of him, ef ye tried from now till next Christmas. Yis, my good woman, I'm John Norton, and this is Wild Bill, and we've come over the mountain to wish ye a merry Christmas, ye and yer leetle uns, and help ye keep the day; and, ye see, we've been stirrin' a leetle in yer absence, and breakfast be waitin'. Wild Bill and me will jest go out and cut a leetle more wood, while ye warm and wash yerself; and. when ye be ready to eat, ye may call us, and we'll see which can git into the house fust."

So saying, the Trapper, followed by his companion, passed out of the door, while the poor woman, without a word, moved toward the fire, and, casting one look at her children, at the table, at the food on the hearthstone, dropped on her knees by a chair, and buried her face in her hands.

"I say," said Wild Bill to the Trapper, as he crept softly away from the door, to which he had returned to shut it more closely, "I say, John Norton, the woman is on her knees by a chair."

"Very likely, very likely," returned the old man reverently; and then he began to chop vigorously at a huge log, with his back toward his comrade.

Perhaps some of you who read this tale will come sometime, when weary and heart-sick, to something drearier than an empty house, some bleak, cold day, some lonely morn, and with a starving heart and benumbed soul,—ay, and empty-handed, too,—enter in only to find it swept and garnished, and what you most needed and longed for waiting for you. Then will you, too, drop upon your knees, and cover your face with your hands, ashamed that you had murmured against the hardness of your lot, or forgotten the goodness of Him who suffered you to be tried only that you might more fully appreciate the triumph.

"My good woman," said the Trapper, when the breakfast was eaten, "we've come, as we said, to spend the day with you; and accordin' to custom—and a pleasant un it be fur sartin—we've brought ye some presents. A good many of them come from him who called on ye as he and me passed through the lake last fall. I dare say ye remember him, and he sartinly has remembered ye. Fur last evenin', when I was makin' up a leetle pack to bring ye myself,—fur I conceited I had better come over and spend the day with ye,—Wild Bill came to my door with a box on his sled that the boy had sent in from his home in the city; and in the box he had put a great many presents fur him and me; and in the lower half of the box he had put a good many presents fur ye and yer leetle uns, and we've brought them all over with us. Some of the things be fur eatin' and some of them be fur wearin'; and that there may be no misunderstanding I would say that all the things that be in the packbasket there, and all the things that be on the sled, too, belong to ye. And as I see the woodpile isn't a very big un fur this time of the year, Bill and me be goin' out to settle our breakfast a leetle with the axes. And while we be gone, I conceit ye had better rummage the things over, and them that be good fur eatin' ye had better put in the cupboard, and them that be good fur wearin' ye had better put on yerself and yer leetle uns; and then we'll all be ready to make a fair start. Fur this be Christmas Day, and we be goin' to keep it as it orter be kept. Ef we've had sorrers, we'll forgit 'em; and we'll laugh, and eat, and be merry. Fur this be Christmas, my good woman! children, this be Christmas! Wild Bill, my boy, this be Christmas; and pups, this be Christmas! And we'll all laugh, and eat, and be merry."

The joyfulness of the old man was contagious. His happiness flowed over as waters flow over the rim of a fountain. Wild Bill laughed as he seized his axe, the woman rose from the table smiling, the girls giggled, the little boy stamped, and the hounds, catching the spirit of their merry master, swung their tails round, and bayed in canine gladness; and amid the joyful uproar the old Trapper spun himself out of the door, and chased Wild Bill through the snow like a boy.

The dinner was to be served at two o'clock; and what a dinner it was, and what preparations preceded! The snow had been shovelled from around the cabin, the holes in the roof roughly but effectually thatched. A good pile of wood was stacked in front of the doorway. The spring that bubbled from the bank had been cleared of ice, and a protection constructed over it. The huge buck had been dressed, and hung high above the reach of wolves. Cedar and balsam branches had been placed in the corners and along the sides of the room. Great sprays of the tasselled pine and the feathery tamarack were suspended from the ceiling. The table had been enlarged, and extra seats extemporized. The long-unused oven had been cleaned out, and under its vast dome the red flames flashed and rolled upward. What a change a few hours had brought to that lonely cabin and its wretched inmates! The woman, dressed in her new garments, her hair smoothly combed, her face lighted with smiles, looked positively comely. The girls, happy in their fine clothes and marvellous toys, danced round the room, wild with delight; while the little boy strutted about the floor in his new boots, proudly showing them to each person for the hundredth time.

The hostess's attention was equally divided between the temperature of the oven and the adornment of the table. A snow-white sheet, one of a dozen she had found in the box, was drafted peremptorily into service, and did duty as a tablecloth. Oh, the innocent and funny make-shifts of poverty, and the goodly distance it can make a little go! Perhaps some of us, as we stand in our rich dining-rooms, and gaze with pride at the silver, the gold, the cut-glass, and the transparent china, can recall a little kitchen in a homely house far away, where our good mothers once set their tables for their guests, and what a brave show the few extra dishes made when they brought them out on the rare festive days!

However it might strike you, fair reader, to the poor woman and her guests there was nothing incongruous in a sheet serving as a tablecloth. Was it not white and clean and properly shaped, and would it not have been a tablecloth if it hadn't been a sheet? How very nice and particular some people can be over the trifling matter of a name! And this sheet had no right to be a sheet; for any one with half an eye could see at a glance that it was predestined from the first to be a tablecloth, for it sat as smoothly on the wooden surface as pious looks on a deacon's face, while the easy and nonchalant way it draped itself at the corners was perfectly jaunty.

The edges of this square of white sheeting that had thus providentially found its true and predestined use were ornamented with the leaves of the wild myrtle, stitched on in the form of scallops. In the centre, with a brave show of artistic skill, were the words, "Merry Christmas," prettily worked with the small brown cones of the pines. This, the joint product of Wild Bill's' industry and the woman's taste, commanded the enthusiastic admiration of all; and even the little boy, from the height of a chair into which he had climbed, was profoundly affected by the show it made.

The Trapper had charge of the meat department, and it is safe to say that no Delmonico could undertake to serve venison in greater variety than did he. To him it was a grand occasion, and—in a culinary sense—he rose grandly to meet it. What bosom is without its little vanities? and shall we laugh at the dear old man because he looked upon the opportunity before him with feeling other than pure benevolence,—even of complacency that what he was doing was being done as no one else could do it?

There was venison roasted, and venison broiled, and venison fried; there was hashed venison, and venison spitted; there was a side-dish of venison sausage, strong with the odor of sage, and slightly dashed with wild thyme; and a huge kettle of soup, on whose rich creamy surface pieces of bread and here and there a slice of potato floated.

"I tell ye, Bill," said the Trapper to his companion, as he stirred the soup with a long ladle, "this pot isn't actilly runnin' over with taters, but ye can see a bit occasionally ef ye look sharp and keep the ladle goin' round pretty lively. No, the taters ain't over-plenty," continued the old man, peering into the pot, and sinking his voice to a whisper, "but there wasn't but fifteen in the bag, and the woman took twelve of 'em fur her kittle, and ye can't make three taters look actilly crowded in two gallons of soup, can ye, Bill?" And the old man punched that personage in the ribs with the thumb of the hand that was free from service, while he kept the ladle going with the other.

"Lord!" exclaimed the Trapper, speaking to Bill, who, having taken a look into the old man's kettle, was digging his knuckles into his eyes to free them from the spray that was jetted into them from the fountains of mirth within that were now in full play,—"Lord! ef there isn't another piece of tater gone all to pieces! Bill, ef I make another circle with this ladle, there won't be a whole slice left, and ye'll swear there wasn't a tater in the soup." And the two men, with their faces within twenty inches, laughed and laughed like boys.

How sweet it is to think that when the Maker set up this strange instrument we call ourselves, and strung it for service, he selected of the heavy chords so few, and of the lighter ones so many! Some muffled ones there are; some slow and solemn sounds swell sadly forth at intervals, but blessed be God that we are so easily tickled, and the world is so funny that within it, even when exiled from home and friends, we find, as the days come and go, the causes and occasions of hilarity!

Wild Bill had been placed in charge of the liquids. What a satire there is in circumstances, and how those of to-day laugh at those of yesterday! Yes, Wild Bill had charge of the liquids,—no mean charge, when the occasion is considered. Nor was the position without its embarrassments, as few honorable positions are, for it brought him face to face with the problem of the day—dishes;

for, between the two cooks of the occasion, every dish in the cabin had been brought into requisition, and poor Bill was left in the predicament of having to make tea and coffee with no pots to make them in.

But Bill was not lacking in wit, if he was in pots, and he solved the conundrum how to make tea without a teapot in a manner that extorted the woman's laughter, and commanded the old Trapper's admiration.

In ransacking the lofts above the apartment, he had lighted on several large, stone jugs, which, with the courage—shall we call it the audacity?—of genius, he had seized upon; and, having thoroughly rinsed them, and freed them from certain odors,—which we are free to say Bill was more or less familiar with,—he brought them forward as substitutes for kettle and pot. Indeed, they worked admirably, for in them the berry and the leaves might not only be properly steeped, but the flavor could be retained beyond what it might in many of our famous and high-sounding patented articles.

But Bill, while ingenious and courageous to the last degree, was lacking in education, especially in scientific directions. He had never been made acquainted with that great promoter of modern civilization—the expansive properties of steam. The corks he had whittled out for his bravely extemporized tea and coffee pots were of the closest fit; and, as they had been inserted with the energy of a man who, having conquered a serious difficulty, is determined to reap the full benefit of his triumph, there was at least no danger that the flavor of the concoctions would escape through any leakage at the muzzle. Having thus prepared them for steeping, he placed the jugs in his corner of the fireplace, and pushed them well up through the ashes to the live coals.

"Wild Bill," said the Trapper, who wished to give his companion the needed warning in as delicate and easy a manner as possible, "Wild Bill, ye have sartinly got the right idee techin' the makin' of tea and coffee, fur the yarb should be steeped, and the berry too,—leastwise, arter it's biled up once or twice,—and therefore it be only reasonable that the nozzles should be closed moderately tight; but a man wants considerable experience in the business, or he's likely to overdo it jest a leetle, and ef ye don't cut some slots in them wooden corks ye've driven into them nozzles, Bill, there'll be a good deal of tea and coffee floatin' round in your comer of the fireplace afore many minutes, and I conceit there'll be a man about your size lookin' for a couple of corks and pieces of jugs out there in the clearin', too."

"Do you think so?" answered Bill incredulously. "Don't you be scared, old man, but keep on stirring your soup and turning the meat, and I'll keep my eye on the bottles."

"That's right, Bill," returned the Trapper; "ye keep yer eye right on 'em, specially on that un that's furderest in toward the butt of the beech log there; fur ef there's any vartue in signs, that jug be gittin' oneasy. Yis," continued the old man, after a minute's pause, during which his eye hadn't left the jug, "yis, that jug will want more room afore many minutes, ef I'm any jedge, and I conceit I had better give it the biggest part of the fireplace;" and the Trapper hastily moved the soup and his half-dozen plates of cooked meats to the other end of the hearthstone, whither he retired himself, like one who, feeling that he is called upon to contend with unknown forces, wisely beats a retreat. He even put himself behind a stack of wood that lay piled up in his corner, like one who does not despise, in a sudden emergency, an artificial protection.

"Bill," called the Trapper, "edge round a leetle,—edge round, and git in closer to the jamb. It's sheer foolishness standin' where ye be, fur the water will be wallopin' in a minit, and ef the corks be swelled in the nozzle, there'll be an explosion. Git in toward the jamb, and watch the ambushment under kiver."

"Old man," answered Bill, as he turned his back carelessly toward the fireplace, "I've got the bearin's of this trail, and know what I'm about. The jugs are as strong as iron kittles, and I ain't afraid of their bust"—

Bill never finished the sentence, for the explosion predicted by the Trapper occurred. It was a tremendous one, and the huge fireplace was filled with flying brands, ashes, and clouds of steam. The Trapper ducked his head, the woman screamed, and the hounds rushed howling to the farthest end of the room; while Bill, with half a somersault, disappeared under the table.

"Hurrah!" shouted the Trapper, lifting his head from behind the wood, and critically surveying the scene. "Hurrah, Bill!" he shouted, as he swung the ladle over his head. "Come out from under the table, and man yer battery agin. Yer old mortars was loaded to the muzzle, and ef ye had depressed the pieces a leetle, ye'd 'a' blowed the cabin to splinters; as it was, the chimney got the biggest part of the chargin', and ye'll find yer rammers on the other side of the mountain."

It was, in truth, a scene of uproarious hilarity; for once the explosion was over, and the woman and children saw there was no danger, and apprehended the character of the performance, they joined unrestrainedly in the Trapper's laughter, in which they were assisted by Wild Bill, as if he were not the victim of his own over-confidence.

"I say, old Trapper," he called from under the table, "did both guns go off? I was gitting under cover when the battery opened, and didn't notice whether the firing was in sections or along the whole line. If there's a piece left, I think I will stay where I am; for I am in a good position to observe the range, and watch the effect of the shot. I say, hadn't you better get behind the wood-pile again?"

"No, no," interrupted the Trapper; "the whole battery went at the word, Bill, and there isn't a gun or a gun-carriage left in the casement. Ye've wasted a gill of the yarb, and a quarter of a pound of the berry; and ye must hurry up with another outfit of bottles, or we'll have nothin' but water to drink at the dinner."

The dinner! That great event of the day, the crown and diadem to its royalty, and which became it so well, was ready promptly to the hour. The table, enlarged as it was to nearly double its original dimensions, could scarcely accommodate the abundance of the feast. Ah, if some sweet power would only enlarge our hearts when, on festive days, we enlarge our tables, how many of the world's poor, that now go hungry while we feast, would then be fed!

At one end of the table sat the Trapper, Wild Bill at the other. The woman's chair was at the centre of one of the sides, so that she sat facing the fire, whose generous flames might well symbolize the abundance which amid cold and hunger had so suddenly come to her. On her right hand the two girls sat; on her left, the boy. A goodly table, a goodly fire, and a goodly company,—what more could the Angel of Christmas ask to see?

Thus were they seated, ready to begin the repast; but the plates remained untouched, and the happy noises which had to that moment filled the cabin ceased; for the Angel of Silence, with noiseless step, had suddenly entered the room. There's a silence of grief, there's a silence of hatred, there's a silence of dread; of these, men may speak, and these they can describe. But the silence of our happiness, who can describe that? When the heart is full, when the long longing is suddenly met, when love gives to love abundantly, when the soul lacketh nothing and is content,— then language is useless, and the Angel of Silence becomes our only adequate interpreter. A humble table, surely, and humble folk around it; but not in the houses of the rich or the palaces of kings does gratitude find her only home, but in more lowly abodes and with lowly folk—ay, and often at the scant table, too—she sitteth a perpetual guest. Was it memory? Did the Trapper at that brief moment visit his absent friend? Did Wild Bill recall his wayward past? Were the thoughts of the woman busy with sweet scenes of earlier days? And did memory, by thus reminding them of the absent and the past, of the sweet things that had been and were, stir within their hearts thoughts of Him from whom all gifts descend, and of His blessed Son, in whose honor the day was named?

O memory! thou tuneful bell that ringeth on forever, friend at our feasts, and friend, too, let us call thee, at our burial, what music can equal thine? For in thy mystic globe all tunes abide,— the birthday note for kings, the marriage peal, the funeral knell, the gleeful jingle of merry mirth, and those sweet chimes that float our thoughts, like fragrant ships upon a fragrant sea, toward heaven,—all are thine! Ring on, thou tuneful bell; ring on, while these glad ears may drink thy melody; and when thy chimes are heard by me no more, ring loud and clear above my grave that peal which echoes to the heavens, and tells the world of immortality, that they who come to mourn. may check their tears, and say, *"Why do we weep? He liveth still!"*

"The Lord be praised fur his goodness!" said the Trapper, whose thoughts unconsciously broke into speech. "The Lord be praised fur his goodness, and make us grateful fur his past marcies, and the plenty that be here!" And looking down upon the viands spread before him, he added, "The Lord be good to the boy, and make him as happy in his city home as be they who be wearin' and eatin' his gifts in the woods!"

"Amen!" said the woman softly, and a grateful tear fell on her plate.

"A—hem!" said Wild Bill; and then looking down upon his warm suit, he lifted his voice, and bringing it out in a clear, strong tone, said, *"Amen! hit or miss!"*

At many a table that day more formal grace was said, by priest and layman alike, and at many a table, by lips of old and young, response was given to the benediction; but we doubt if over all the earth a more honest grace was said or assented to than the Lord heard from the cabin in the woods.

The feast and the merry-making now began. The old Trapper was in his best mood, and fairly bubbled over with humor. The wit of Wild Bill was naturally keen, and it flashed at its best as he ate. The children stuffed and laughed as only children on such an elastic occasion can. And as for the poor woman, it was impossible for her, in the midst of such a scene, to be otherwise than happy, and she joined modestly in the conversation, and laughed heartily at the witty sallies.

But why should we strive to put on paper the wise, the funny, and the pleasant things that were said, the exclamations, the laughter, the story, the joke, the verbal thrust and parry of such an occasion? These, springing from the centre of the circumstance, and flashed into being at the instant, cannot be preserved for after-rehearsal. Like the effervescence of champagne, they jet and are gone; their force passes away with the noise that accompanied its out-coming.

Is it not enough to record that the dinner was a success, that the Trapper's meats were put upon the table in a manner worthy of his reputation, that the woman's efforts at pastry-making were generously applauded, and that Wild Bill's tea and coffee were pronounced by the hostess the best she had ever tasted? Perhaps no meal was ever more enjoyed, as certainly none was ever more heartily eaten.

The wonder and pride of the table was the pudding,—a creation of Indian-meal, flour, suet, and raisins, re-enforced and assisted by innumerable spicy elements supposed to be too mysterious to be grasped by the masculine mind. In the production of this wonderful centre-piece,—for it had been unanimously voted the place of honor,—the poor woman had summoned all the latent resources of her skill, and in reference to it her pride and fear contended, while the anxiety with which she rose to serve it was only too plainly depicted on her countenance. What if it should prove a failure? What if she had made a miscalculation as to the amount of suet required,—a point upon which she had been somewhat confused? What if the raisins were not sufficiently distributed? What if it wasn't done through, and should turn out pasty? Great

heavens! The last thought was of so overwhelming a character that no feminine courage could encounter it. Who may describe the look with which she watched the Trapper as he tasted it, or the expression of relief which brightened her anxious face when he pronounced warmly in its favor?

"It's a wonderful bit of cookin'," he said, addressing himself to Wild Bill, "and I sartinly doubt ef there be anything in the settlements to-day that can equal it. There be jest enough of the suet, and there be a plum fur every mouthful; and it be solid enough to stay in the mouth ontil ye've had time to chew it, and git a taste of the corn,—and I wouldn't give a cent for a puddin' ef it gits away from yer teeth fast. Yis, it be a wonderful bit of cookin'," and, turning to the woman, he added, "ye may well be proud of it."

What higher praise could be bestowed? And as it was re-echoed by all present, and plate after plate was passed for a second filling, the dinner came to an end with the greatest good feeling and hilarity.

IV.

"Now fur the sled!" exclaimed the Trapper, as he rose from the table. "It be a good many years since I've straddled one, but nothin' settles a dinner quicker, or suits the leetle folks better. I conceit the crust be thick enough to bear us up, and, ef it is, we can fetch a course from the upper edge of the clearin' fifty rods into the lake. Come, childun, git on yer mittens and yer tippets, and h'ist along to the big pine, and ye shall have some fun ye won't forgit ontil yer heads be whiter than mine."

It is needless to record that the children hailed with delight the proposition of the Trapper, or that they were at the appointed spot long before the speaker and his companion reached it with the sled.

"Wild Bill," said the Trapper, as they stood on the crest of the slope down which they were to glide, "the crust be smooth as glass, and the hill be a steep un. I sartinly doubt ef mortal man ever rode faster than this sled'll be goin' by the time it gits to where the bank pitches into the lake; and ef ye should git a leetle careless in yer steerin', Bill, and hit a stump, I conceit that nothin' but the help of the Lord or the rottenness of the stump would save ye from etarnity."

Now, Wild Bill was blessed with a sanguine temperament. To him no obstacle seemed serious if bravely faced. Indeed, his natural confidence in himself bordered on recklessness, to which the drinking habits of his life had, perhaps, contributed.

When the Trapper had finished speaking, Bill ran his eye carelessly down the steep hillside, smooth and shiny as polished steel, and said, "Oh, this isn't anything extry for a hill. I've steered a good many steeper ones, and in nights when the moon was at the half, and the sled overloaded at that. It don't make any difference how fast you go," he added, "if you only keep in the path, and don't hit anything."

"That's it, that's it," replied the Trapper. "But the trouble here be to keep in the path, fur, in the fust place, there isn't any path, and the stumps be pretty thick, and I doubt ef ye can line a trail from here to the bank by the lake without one or more sudden twists in it, and a twist in the trail, goin' as fast as we'll be goin', has got to be taken jediciously, or somethin' will happen. I say, Bill, what p'int will ye steer fur?"

Wild Bill, thus addressed, proceeded to give his opinion touching the proper direction of the flight they were to make. Indeed, he had been closely examining the ground while the Trapper was speaking, and therefore gave his opinion promptly and with confidence.

"Ye have chosen the course with jedgment," said the old man approvingly, after he had studied the line his companion pointed out critically for a moment. "Yis, Bill, ye have a nateral eye for the business, and I sartinly have more confidence in ye than I had a minit ago, when ye was talkin' about a steeper hill than this; fur this hill drops mighty sudden in the pitches, and the crust be smooth as ice, and the sled'll go like a streak when it gits started. But the course ye've p'inted out be a good un, fur there be only one bad turn in it, and good steerin' orter put a sled round that. I say," continued the old man, turning toward his companion, and pointing out the crook in the course at the bottom of the second dip, "can ye swing around that big stump there without upsettin' when ye come to it?"

"Swing around? Of course I can," retorted Wild Bill positively. "There's plenty room to the left, and"—

"Ay, ay; there be plenty of room, as ye say, ef ye don't take too much of it," interrupted the Trapper. "But"—

"I tell you," broke in the other, "I'll turn my back to no man in steering a sled; and I can put this sled, and you on it, around that stump a hundred times, and never lift a runner."

"Well, well," responded the Trapper, "have it your own way. I dare say ye be good at steerin', and I sartinly know I'm good at ridin'; and I can ride as fast as ye can steer, ef ye hit every stump in the clearin'. Now, childun," continued the old man, turning to the little group, "we be goin' to try the course; and ef the crust holds up, and Wild Bill keeps clear of the stumps, and nothin' onusual happens, ye shall have all the slidin' ye want afore ye go in. Come, Bill, git yer sled p'inted right, and I'll be gittin' on, and we'll see ef ye can steer an old man round a stump as handily as ye say ye can."

The directions of the Trapper were promptly obeyed, and in an instant the sled was in a right position, and the Trapper proceeded to seat himself with the carefulness of one who feels he is embarking on a somewhat uncertain venture, and has grave misgivings as to what will be the upshot of the undertaking. The sled was large and strongly built; and it added not a little to his comfort to feel that he could put entire confidence in the structure beneath them.

"The sled'll hold," he said to himself, "ef the loadin' goes to the jedgment."

The Trapper was no sooner seated than Wild Bill threw himself upon the sled, with one leg under him and the other stretched at full length behind. This was a method of steering that had come into vogue since the Trapper's boyhood, for in his day the steersman sat astride the sled, with his feet thrust forward, and steered by the pressure of either heel upon the snow.

"Hold on, Bill!" exclaimed the Trapper, whose eye this novel method of steering had not escaped. "Hold on, and hold up a minit. Heavens and 'arth! ye don't mean to steer this sled with one toe, do ye, and that, too, the length of a rifle-barrel astarn? Wheel round, and spread yer legs out as ye orter, and steer this sled in an honest fashion, or there'll be trouble aboard afore ye git to the bottom."

"Sit round!" retorted Bill. "How could I see to steer if I was sitting right back of you? For you're nigh a foot taller than I be, and your shoulders are as broad as the sled."

"Yer p'ints be well taken, fur sartin," replied the Trapper; "fur it be no more than reasonable that the man that steers should see where he be goin', and I am anxious as ye be that ye should. Yis, I sartinly want ye to see where ye be goin' on this trip, anyhow, fur the crew be a fresh un, and the channel be a leetle crooked. But be ye sartin, Bill, that ye can fetch round that stump there as it orter be did, with nothin' but yer toe out behind? It may be the best way, as ye say, but it don't look like honest steerin' to a man of my years."

"I have used both ways," answered Bill, "and I give you my word, old man, that this is the best one. You can git a big swing with your foot stretched out in this fashion, and the sled feels the least pressure of the toe. Yes, it's all right. John Norton, are you ready?"

"Yis, yis, as ready as I ever shall be," answered the Trapper, in a voice in which doubt and resignation were equally mingled. "It may be as ye say," he continued; "but the rudder be too fur behind to suit me, and ef anything happens on this cruise, jest remember, Wild Bill, that my jedgment"—

The sentence the Trapper was uttering was abruptly cut short at this point; for Bill had started the sled with a sudden push, and leaped to his seat behind the Trapper as it glided downward and away. In an instant the sled was under full headway, for the dip was a sharp one, and the crust smooth as ice. Scarce had it gone ten rods from the point where it started before it was in full flight, and was gliding downward with what would have been, to any but a man of the steadiest nerve, a frightful velocity. But the Trapper was of too cool and courageous temperament to be disturbed even by actual danger. Indeed, the swiftness of their downward career, as the sled with a buzz and a roar swept along over the resounding crust, stirred the old man's blood with a tingle of excitement; while the splendid manner with which Wild Bill was keeping it to the course settled upon filled him with admiration, and was fast making him a convert to the new method of steering.

Downward they flashed. The Trapper's cap had been blown from his head; and as the old man sat bolt-upright on his sled, his feet bravely planted on the round, his face flushed, and his white hair streaming, he looked the very picture of hearty enjoyment. Above his head the face of Wild Bill looked actually sharpened by the pressure of the air on either cheek as it clove through it; but his lips were bravely set, and his eyes were fastened without winking on the big stump ahead, toward which they were rushing.

It was at this point that Wild Bill vindicated his ability as a steersman, and at the same time barely escaped shipwreck. At the proper moment he swept his foot to the left, and the sled, in obedience to the pressure, swooped in that direction. But in his anxiety to give the stump a wide berth, Bill overdid the pressure that was needed a trifle; for in calculating the curve required he had failed to allow for the sidewise motion of the sled, and, instead of hitting one stump, it looked for an instant as if he would be precipitated among a dozen.

"Heave her starn up, Wild Bill' up with her starn, I say," yelled the Trapper, "or there won't be a stump left in the clearin'."

With a quickness and courage that would have done credit to any steersman,—for the speed at which they were going was terrific,—Bill swept his foot to the right, leaning his body well over at the same instant. The Trapper instinctively seconded his endeavors, and with hands that gripped either side of the sled he hung over that side which was upon the point of going into the air. For several rods the sled glided along on a single runner, and then, righting itself with a lurch, jumped the summit of the last dip, and raced away, like a swallow in full flight, toward the lake.

Now, at the edge of the clearing that bounded the shore was a bank of considerable size. Shrubs and stunted bushes fringed the crest of it. These had been buried beneath the snow, and the crust had formed smoothly over them; and as it was upheld by no stronger support than such as the hidden shrubbery furnished, it was incapable of sustaining any considerable pressure.

Certainly no sled was ever moving faster than was Wild Bill's, when it came to this point; and certainly no sled ever stopped quicker, for the treacherous crust dropped suddenly under it, and the sled was left with nothing but the hind part of one of the runners sticking up in sight. But though the sled was suddenly checked in its career, the Trapper and Wild Bill continued their flight. The former slid from the sled without meeting any obstruction, and with the same velocity with which he had been moving. Indeed, so little was his position changed, that one almost might fancy that no accident had happened, and that the old man was gliding forward to the end of the course with an adequate structure under him. But with the latter it was far different; for, as the sled stopped, he was projected sharply upward into the air, and, after turning several somersaults, he actually landed in front of the Trapper, and glided along on the slippery surface ahead of him. And so the two men shot onward, one after the other, while the children cackled from the hill-top, and the woman swung her bonnet over her head, and laughed from her position in the doorway.

"Bill," called the Trapper, when by dint of much effort they had managed to check their motion somewhat, "Bill, ef the cruise be about over, I conceit we'd better anchor hereabouts. But I shipped fur the voyage, and ye be capt'in, and as ye've finally got the right way to steer, I feel pretty safe techin' the futur."

It was not until they had come to a full stop, and looked around them, that they realized the distance they had come; for they had in truth slid nearly across the bay.

"I've boated a good many times on these waters, and under sarcumstances that called fur 'arnest motion, but I sartinly never went across this bay as fast as I've did it to-day. How do ye feel, Bill, how do ye feel?"

"A good deal shaken up," was the answer, "a good deal shaken up."

"I conceit as much," answered the Trapper, "I conceit as much, fur ye left the sled with mighty leetle deliberation; and when I saw yer legs cornin' through the air, I sartinly doubted ef the ice would hold ye. But ye steered with jedgment; yis, ye steered with jedgment, Bill; and I'd said it ef we'd gone to the bottom."

The sun was already set when they returned to the cabin; for, selecting a safer course, they had given the children an hour's happy sliding. The woman had prepared some fresh tea and a lunch, which they ate with lessened appetites, but with humor that never flagged. When it was ended, the old Trapper rose to depart, and with a dignity and tenderness peculiarly his own, thus spoke:—

"My good woman," he said, "the moon will soon be up, and the time has come fur me to be goin'. I've had a happy day with ye and the leetle uns; and the trail over the mountain will seem shorter, as the pups and me go home, thinkin' on't. Wild Bill will

stay a few days, and put things a leetle more to rights, and git up
a wood-pile that will keep ye from choppin' fur a good while. It's
his own thought, and ye can thank him accordin'ly." Then, having
kissed each of the children, and spoken a few words to Wild Bill,
he took the woman's hand, and said,—

"The sorrers of life be many, but the Lord never forgits. I've
lived ontil my head be whitenin', and I've noted that though
he moves slowly, he fetches most things round about the time
we need 'em ; and the things that be late in cornin', I conceit we
shall git somewhere furder on. Ye didn't kill the big buck this
mornin', but the meat ye needed hangs at yer door, nevertheless."
And, shaking the woman heartily by the hand, he whistled to the
hounds, and passed out of the door. The inmates of the cabin stood
and watched him, until, having climbed the slope of the clearing,
he disappeared in the shadows of the forest; and then they closed
the door. But more than once Wild Bill noted that as the woman
stood wiping her dishes, she wiped her eyes as well; and more
than once he heard her say softly to herself, "God bless the dear
old man!

Ay, ay, poor woman, we join thee in thy prayer. God bless the
dear old man! and not only him, but all who do the deeds he did.
God bless them one and all!

Over the crusted snow the Trapper held his course, until he
came, with a happy heart, to his cabin. Soon a fire was burning
on his own hearthstone, and the hounds were in their accustomed
place. He drew the table in front, where the fire's fine light fell
on his work, and, taking some green vines and branches from
the basket, began to twine a wreath. One he twined, and then he
began another; and often, as he twined the fadeless branches in,
he paused, and long and lovingly looked at the two pictures hanging on the wall; and when the wreaths were twined, he hung them
on the frames, and, standing in front of the dumb reminders of his
absent ones, he said, *"I miss them, so!"*

Ah! friend, dear friend, when life's glad day with you and me is
passed, when the sweet Christmas chimes are rung for other ears
than ours, when other hands set the green branches up, and other

feet glide down the polished floor, may there be those still left behind to twine us wreaths, and say, *"We miss them so!"*

And this is the way John Norton the Trapper kept his Christmas.

9

CAMPING

There is no other word in the vocabulary of our language so suggestive of rare and pleasant conditions of living as camping. It is more than a mere word; it is a symbol as well. It stands for a class of experiences so fresh, novel, and healthy that it is beloved by imagination and memory alike. It is so truly a mirror to many of us that in it, as in a glass, we see trees, the shores of lovely lakes, the banks of quietly flowing rivers, wooded islands around which the waves run caressingly, beaches of gleaming sand, and ranges of lofty mountains. In it, also, are cabins of bark, camp-fires that crackle, and blaze, and flare red lights high up amid swaying branches, and widely out in a great circle through the dark forest. And in the word are faces and forms that have been companions with us in our forest wanderings, some of whom are with us to this day, and other ones that are not now with us, nor will they ever be again on this earth, and, alas! we know not where they arc.

Not only is it a word for the eye, but it is equally a word for the ear. For in it are the sighing of zephyrs, the soft intoning of slow-moving night winds, the roaring of strong gales, the moaning of tempests, and the sobbings of storms among the wet trees. The loon's call, the splash of leaping fish, the panther's cry, the pitiful summons of the lost hound, the slashing of deer wading among the lily pads, and the soft dripping of odorous gums falling gently on the pine stems, listening to which in silence and sweet content, we, who were lying under the fragrant trees, like happy and weary children, have fallen gently asleep,—all these sounds live in the word as music lives forever in the air of heaven, being a part of it.

And in it too are human voices, songs, laughter, and all the happy noises of merriment and frolic. No other phonograph is like to it. The happy hunter's proud hurrah over the captured game; the songs around the camp-fire under the stars in the hush of evening; the stranger's hail; the guide's strong call to breakfast, a heavenly sound—the flute's soft note across the water on a still night; the cheer on reaching camp, and the murmured farewells at leaving; verily, it is a vocal word, and all the sounds that come from it are melody.

Dear word, sweet word, keep vocal to my ears until they cease to hear, and mirror to my eyes until they see no more the fair, the sweet, and the honest faces that out of the dear old camps that we have builded in so many parts for so many years, now look forth upon me as out of many heavens. For if there be a better heaven than a well-placed camp with a wisely assorted company of honest and cheerful folk, I know not how to find it in my imagination nor that passage of Revelation that tells us of it.

CPSIA information can be obtained
at www.ICGtesting.com
Printed in the USA
LVHW110435121022
730468LV00005B/235